THE
BLACK
LENS

THE BLACK LENS

CHRISTOPHER STOLLAR

Boyle
&
Dalton

Book Design & Production
Columbus Publishing Lab
www.ColumbusPublishingLab.com

Paperback ISBN 978-1-63337-072-2
Hardback ISBN 978-1-63337-076-0
E-book ISBN 978-1-63337-071-5

Printed in the United States of America
1 3 5 7 9 10 8 6 4 2

To Mom, who kindled my love for writing.
To my wife, who kept those embers burning.
And to everybody who torched my drafts
until one survived the fire.

Bleak, dark and piercing cold,
It was a night for the well housed and fed
to draw round the bright fire …
And for the homeless starving wretch
to lay him down and die.

— Charles Dickens —

THE
FOCUS

CHAPTER 1

When Zoey James looked at the scar below her left eye, she thought of her dad.

That bastard could go to hell for all she cared. Every time she remembered him she felt trapped inside her own body. But Zoey knew she couldn't think about that anymore. Not now. Because tonight she had to be strong for her sister.

So Zoey smeared on a dark mass of eyeliner. As usual, extra thick. Especially beneath her left lid. She didn't bother to fuss with any other makeup or even her hair. Instead, Zoey hid the brown mess beneath her black hoodie. She grabbed the only pair of jeans she owned, still stained with ketchup. Her mom couldn't afford the Laundromat this week. Once again.

While Zoey laced up her old steel-toed boots, her sister Camille walked into the room.

"How's this?" Camille asked.

Zoey cringed when she saw her sister wearing a Snow White sweatshirt filled with holes.

"You can't wear that," Zoey said.

"Why not?" Camille asked. "Camille loves Snow White."

"I know, but you can't wear a shirt like that to a party."

Zoey heard a horn honk outside their trailer.

"Come on, Camille. Mom's waiting."

As her sister found another sweater, Zoey stepped into the kitchen. She searched for food, but saw only a red apple rotting behind piles of dishes. Zoey reached for the door, almost forgetting to tell Quill goodbye. She ran to her cage. It was open.

Not again, Zoey thought.

Her mom blasted the horn this time. Camille came back out with a Cinderella sweatshirt that looked a little better, but still childish. While her sister grabbed some gloves, Zoey searched one last time for her pet. She peeked behind the space heater that hummed in the corner. She eyed the windowsills stuffed with blankets to keep the warm air from escaping. And she even checked on top of the TV that rested upon plastic clothes hampers.

Quill wasn't in her usual spots, but they had to leave. Zoey brushed Camille's frizzy hair back into a ponytail. Then the two sisters raced out the flimsy aluminum door that never quite slammed shut and stood by their mom's old Toyota Corolla.

"Sorry, Quill escaped again," Zoey told her mom, Ella.

Ella shook her head as she put another chunk of chewing tobacco into her mouth and then spit into a plastic cup.

"I don't care," her mom said. "You know we've got to leave before your dad gets home. Just trying to keep you girls safe."

Zoey nodded, but her sister hesitated.

"Mom, can we just take the car by ourselves tonight?"

Camille asked. "We'll be back before midnight."

Ella looked skeptical. She glanced back and forth between her daughters.

"Please Mom," Camille said.

Ella spit into her plastic cup again and then got out of the Corolla. "Fine, but you'd better be back on time."

As Ella tossed the keys to Zoey, she grabbed her sleeve and whispered.

"You keep looking out for your sister, you hear? I'm scared shitless for her. That case manager keeps saying she's been doing fine at a normal school, but I'm not so sure about a party. Promise me you'll protect her tonight."

Zoey nodded. Then she tightened her hoodie and got into the car with Camille. The sisters drove in silence to the party as snow began to fall on Central Oregon. Sometimes Zoey couldn't stand this stupid weather. Last fall the high desert sun burned her pale skin, but this winter came early and was already bringing a chill she had never felt as a little girl. And yet, that kind of violent weather change was typical for such a small, rural town hidden in the shadows of the Cascade Mountain Range and isolated from the rest of Oregon.

Her thoughts turned to dread when they drove past the sign for South County High. The building looked worn and tired. Like their shit-hole town. La Pine probably still had only 1,000 people, maybe even fewer after the Recession. Zoey still couldn't believe this was just the beginning of her junior year and Camille's start as a freshman.

When they got to the party, Zoey wished she had never come.

The loud thump of music blaring from Leah Colson's house reminded Zoey why she hated parties. For her, it was worse than the school cafeteria. At least during lunch she could sit by herself and disappear. But at a party, nobody could hide, especially not around that Leah slut. She was one of the popular girls, after all, and she always threw parties whenever her parents weren't around. That seemed to be every other weekend. Or more.

"Hey girls," Leah said as she opened the door. "Just getting started."

Leah brought them inside and took a swig of something from a plastic red cup that made her teeter on her high heels. Then she led them to the living room, where Zoey could smell vodka, feel hip hop vibrating through her bones and watch pimple-faced boys grind on girls to the beat.

"Want a drink?" Leah asked.

"What?" Zoey shouted. She could barely hear Leah over the music.

"I said, want a drink?"

Zoey shook her head. Leah ignored her and brought them something anyway. Camille took a few gulps, but Zoey only had a couple sips. Tasted like cheap vodka and Gatorade. She felt sick. Dizzy. For a long time, Zoey just stood there drinking and staring at the crowd. Everybody was dancing. Everybody but her.

If it wasn't for the fact that Camille craved acceptance and had bugged her all week about the party, Zoey would have never come here.

"Ready to go?" Zoey asked Camille.

Zoey turned around. Camille wasn't there. She was feeling dizzier by the second, and the black lights made her head spin. Zoey stumbled through the half-naked dancers and into the kitchen where Leah was guzzling down a second cup of liquor.

"Where's Camille?"

Leah didn't say a word. She just pointed upstairs to a dark hallway. Zoey staggered back through the crowd and tripped up the stairs. In the blackness she could hear moaning. At first it sounded like someone was in pain, but then she saw two people in bed with the door open. They kept going even as Zoey walked past them. Down the hall, Zoey heard some more noises coming from one of the rooms. Screams. Maybe. She opened the door, but just found two others in bed.

"Sorry," she said, slamming the door shut.

Zoey felt like she could fall onto the floor, but she continued walking down the hall until she reached the last room. Zoey paused for a second. Nothing. Then she opened it. On the bed lay Camille. Passed out. Naked. Before Zoey could help her sister, her vision blurred and she blacked out.

The pungent smell of a permanent marker forced Zoey to wake up.

She didn't know where it was coming from, but the smell reeked so bad it made her head hurt. As her eyes began to adjust to the dark room, she saw Camille lying next to her on the same bed. Still naked. Camille's body was covered in black marker. Someone had sketched crude pictures of penises on her skin—everywhere except for her face and neck.

"Oh my God," Zoey said as she shook her sister. "Camille, are you OK?"

Camille didn't move. Zoey shook harder. Her sister's cold body remained frozen.

"Wake up, Camille. Please, don't do this to me."

All of a sudden, Camille jerked and rolled over with a groan.

Zoey hugged her sister. "Thank God. What happened?"

Instead of answering, Camille stared at Zoey in horror.

"Zoey, what happened?" Camille asked. "What'd they do?"

Camille pointed to Zoey's body. She looked down in shock. Her own body was also covered in black marker. But instead of pictures, words were scribbled on her breasts and right above her pubic hair:

Slut.
Cunt.
Whore.

Camille started crying. Then she flapped her hands, rocked back and forth and repeated the phrase she often spoke in distress: "It's OK Camille, you're OK. It's OK Camille, you're OK."

As usual, Zoey calmed Camille, gently holding her sister's head in her hands.

"Look at me," Zoey said. "We're going to be OK. But we've got to get the hell out of here."

Zoey helped her sister get dressed and then led her down the steps. The smell of vodka and Gatorade still hung in the air, but the house was silent. Most people were passed out on couches or the floor.

They got into their car and started driving home. Zoey tried to remember what had happened, but only vague images came into her mind. She had never felt this way before. Someone must have slipped something into their drinks.

Her phone buzzed with a text message. Zoey didn't recognize the number, but what she saw made her swerve onto the side of the road:

Ur sisters hot.

Zoey stopped the car. She saw an attached picture of Camille on the bed, wearing nothing but her panties.

Ur even hotter.

The second text showed Zoey in a similar position, but she was completely naked. Zoey thought about not sharing those messages with Camille. But she also knew that could make the situation worse.

"We've got to tell Mom," Zoey said, showing the texts to her sister. "She'll know what to do."

Just then, a final text came through:

If u tell ur mom about the pics, Ill beat ur sister.

A Snapchat photo came through that showed a bruised face of a young girl, who couldn't be much older than them. Zoey thought it looked a little like Leah, but the face was too swollen to tell for sure.

As the picture faded from her phone, Zoey felt sick to her stomach. Someone had touched her body. Someone she didn't know had seen her naked. And this bastard was now threatening to hurt her sister if she didn't obey.

"What'd the last text say?" Camille asked.

Zoey didn't answer. She just headed home in silence.

Camille was fast asleep in the passenger seat when they got back to their trailer.

Zoey gently shook her sister's arm, but that made her jerk awake in shock. Camille flailed her arms and tried scratching the black marker off of them with her long fingernails. She dug deep into her skin. Bruising the flesh.

"Stop," Zoey said, grabbing her sister's hands. "You're going to hurt yourself again. Now listen to me, when we go inside, don't say anything to Mom. Let me do the talking, OK? And keep your sleeves down so she doesn't see the marker."

Camille nodded.

"Good," Zoey said. "Let's go."

They tried creeping into the trailer, but their mom was pacing the floor with the lamp on.

"You're late," Ella said. "Why didn't you girls text me?"

Zoey saw Camille staring at her, waiting for an answer.

"Sorry Mom," Zoey said. "It's my fault. I lost track of time."

Her mom stared at them suspiciously. "What were you doing at the party?"

Zoey shrugged her shoulders.

"Camille, what were you doing?" Ella asked.

Camille looked at Zoey and then stared at the floor. Zoey knew she had to do something. She had to tell her mom everything. The drinks. The drugs. And especially those photos. But then Zoey remembered that last text:

If u tell ur mom about the pics, Ill beat ur sister.

"We were drinking," Zoey said. "I'm sorry. It's my fault, not Camille's."

Ella sighed, embraced her daughters and held them on the couch. The three just sat there for a while, listening to the space heater hum.

"I forgive you," Ella said. "Just promise me you girls won't ever do that again."

They both agreed. Their mom held them tighter as she stroked their hair and sang them a song Zoey hadn't heard in years:

> *This little light of mine,*
> *I'm gonna let it shine,*
> *Let it shine.*
> *Let it shine.*
> *Let it shine.*

"You remember that song?" Ella asked her daughters. "I used to sing that to you girls when you were little. Helped you fall asleep, especially on really cold nights when the space heater was broke."

Zoey smiled as she remembered those moments with her mom. She could still feel those rough yet kind hands massaging her to sleep.

But for the first time, Zoey didn't know if their mom could help.

CHAPTER 2

When Aidan looked at his camera lens, he thought of his boss. That bastard could go to hell for all he cared. Every time he remembered him he felt trapped in his dead-end job. But Aidan knew he couldn't think about that anymore. Not now. Because today he was already running late for the annual Pet Parade.

So Aidan wiped a black speck of dirt from his camera. As usual, extra clean. Especially his long-focus, telephoto lens. He only strode a few blocks before animals began to appear on Bond Street in Bend, a wealthy ski resort community about thirty minutes north of La Pine. Clothed in tiny costumes that matched their owners, the pets marched together on an early winter day at Central Oregon's popular parade. Another "breaking story" for the paper. Maybe even front page. God, it was going to be a long day.

"There's Cat Woman," Aidan said.

He pointed the person out to fellow reporter Cal Townsend while peering through his black, vintage-framed glasses to snap rapid-fire photos. He adjusted the focus. Took a shot. And then adjusted the shutter speed on his Nikon. The harsh, high desert light was killing him.

"And of course, here comes the French Maid," Aidan added with a smirk. He motioned to an old woman who dressed in the same attire each year with her pug. The dog looked strangely like her, but cuter.

"Bro, why do we have to cover this again?" Cal asked while taking notes about a Chihuahua dressed like Superman, suspended in the air by dozens of balloons.

Aidan shook his head. "Cause we've got nothing but bullshit to put on the front page tomorrow. It's days like these I wish we'd have a mass suicide—or at least a robbery. I want some real news for once."

He dropped to one knee and captured a few snouts slobbering past him at eye level. Then he darted across the street to climb on top of a park bench and capture a bird's eye view of the entire crowd.

Despite the stupidity of this event, Aidan loved the thrill of the shoot. He lived for the adrenaline rush of having only one chance to capture that perfect moment in time. One second too late and that shot—that little piece of history—was lost forever.

After taking several more photos, Aidan got a phone call from their editor.

"Where the hell are you guys?"

"Still at your parade, Mitch."

"Well, get your asses to Sixth and Burnside. Cops are reporting gun shots over the scanner, right by the high school."

"Probably nothing again," Aidan said.

He took a couple more shots of animals and then hopped into his Subaru Hatchback with Cal. Aidan grabbed a Clorox wipe from the glove box. He cleaned the dashboard, steering wheel and five pre-set radio buttons.

"Missed a spot," Cal said, pointing to the dashboard. "I'll pay you five bucks not to clean it. Or would that drive your OCD crazy?"

Aidan stared at the speck of dirt, probably left over from their mountain biking trip together last weekend. For a brief moment he tried to let it go. But Aidan couldn't stand any amount of dirt or disorder. So he scrubbed the smudge off. Then he tidied his curly black hair and stroked his razor-trimmed beard.

"Go to hell," Aidan told Cal with a smile.

The two drove with the windows down in comfortable silence, the woodsy smell of juniper and pine wafting through the car. Aidan took the opportunity to light one of his Natural American Spirit cigarettes. Cal followed suit, but with his briar pipe and Black Cavendish tobacco that smelled like rum and vanilla.

"You look like a goddam hobbit," Aidan said.

"Hey, at least I've got class. So, you and Reina still looking at jobs in Seattle or what?"

"Every day," Aidan said. "Especially when I have to shoot stories like the Pet Parade. Nothing ever happens in this hell hole."

Cal puffed on his pipe. "Well, I hope you find something. Just don't be too upset if nothing comes up. Papers all across the country are laying photographers off."

"I know," Aidan said. "I just need a break. I'm tired of covering the same shit."

"You're preaching to the choir, bro. Hey, maybe this 'shooting' will be our first real crime story."

Aidan rolled his mahogany brown eyes. Then he saw flashing lights in front of them. As they got closer, Aidan saw police talking to two teenagers surrounded by reporters from the local TV station. They parked the car and ran up to one of the officers.

"Slow day at the newsroom, huh?" the cop asked. "Unfortunately, it's not much news for you. These boys just set off some illegal fireworks."

"I'm going to kill Mitch," Aidan said.

After getting a few shots, he and Cal headed back to The Cascade Times newsroom. Aidan sighed as he sat down at his desk. As usual, he hung up his North Face jacket and rolled up his white sleeves. He carefully placed his black pen to the left of him, on top of his white reporter's notebook. Finally, he put his tattered leather satchel to the right of his laptop where he could see it.

"What the hell took so long?" his editor barked behind him.

"Goddam it," Aidan said, jumping in surprise and staring at his boss, infamously known for that untrimmed mustache which seemed to creep deeper each day into the caverns of his mouth. "What took so long? You mean, aside from getting some great shots of the French Maid and chasing a shooting that turned out to be nothing but fireworks? Oh, I almost forgot about the five beers we drank on the way back to–"

"Fuck you," Mitch interrupted. "Look, this town may not have as much breaking news as Portland or Seattle, but there are still some good human interest stories here."

"What, like the parade?" Aidan asked. "You're kidding me. That's got to be the lamest excuse for a news story, other than your yearly obsession with potholes. Nobody reads that shit."

"Look, Ade, just give me a damn shot of the parade— I'll let you go."

"Just promise me you won't put those photos anywhere near the front page."

Mitch agreed. Aidan finished his photos over a cup of cold newsroom coffee, threw his satchel over his shoulder and started storming toward the exit before Cal caught up with him.

"Hey, what's wrong?" Cal asked.

"Oh, you know, another fight with Mitch."

"I still can't believe he lets you talk to him like that. Most editors would have fired your ass by now."

"Yeah, but most editors don't have a photographer who also knows how to report," Aidan said. "You know how many times I've covered his ass when somebody screwed up or missed deadline. He owes me."

Cal nodded. "Hey, you still meeting up with us at Deschutes?"

Aidan had almost forgotten about their happy hour at Bend's most popular micro-brewery, renowned for its Black Butte Porter and Mirror Pond Pale Ale.

"Aren't you and Jess coming over tonight?" Aidan asked. "I need to get home to help Reina with dinner. Maybe next week."

"Come on, bro. Just have one drink with us. Briggs will be there. And I heard he may actually have a tip for us this time. Something big."

"All right, one. See you there."

As Aidan walked out of the newsroom, he glanced over at the copy desk to see how they were laying out the front page for tomorrow morning:

Pugs, poodles, people play together at annual Pet Parade.

ad story, with his French Maid photo front

nuttered under his breath.

———

Once Aidan and Cal got to Deschutes Brewery, they huddled in a dark corner by a fireplace and ordered a couple pints of their favorite brew, the Jubelale. Tasted like Christmas.

"God that's good," Aidan said, taking off his glasses and wiping them down. He waved to a man who entered the brick pub. With his buzzed head and huge arms, Randy Briggs looked like a bodybuilder. He was one of the few sheriff's deputies in town who despised doughnuts.

"Ade, you look like shit," Briggs said.

The deputy grabbed a Bud Light from the bartender and then plopped down next to them on an old wooden bench by the fire.

"Another slow day at the newsroom?" Briggs asked.

"I don't even want to talk about it," Aidan said, staring at the deputy's drink. "Also, I can't believe you still drink that shit. It tastes like cat piss. Think it's time you grow up."

"Yeah, but Bud still costs half the price of your cocky-ass drink," the deputy replied. "And it doesn't feel like I'm drinking a loaf of bread."

The friends laughed and clinked their glasses together. Aidan had worked with Cal and Briggs so long he almost thought of them as brothers. And like brothers, they fought and bickered with each other constantly.

"So, what'd you cover today?" Briggs asked.

Aidan explained both the Pet Parade and illegal fireworks. Then they ordered another round of beers and stared into the fire for a while.

Finally, Aidan broke the silence. "So, what do you have for us? Cal said you may have a big tip."

Briggs looked nervously around the room and then motioned for them to lean in closer.

"Promise this is off the record?" Briggs asked.

"Of course."

Briggs took a deep breath. "It's our sheriff. We caught him..."

The deputy looked away.

"Come on," Aidan said. "Look, man, I need something. Anything. I'm growing restless."

"We caught him eating three doughnuts the other day instead of his usual two," Briggs said. "What do you think? Front page? Above the fold?"

Aidan flipped Briggs off. "I hate you. And I hate this goddam town."

"Come on, man," Briggs said. "It's fucking Bend. You really think there's anything big going on here? But at least I got a free beer out of it, right?"

Aidan shook his head and glanced at his watch.

"Damn it, I've got to go," he said, grabbing his jacket and standing up. "Sorry guys, I need to help Reina get dinner ready."

Taking one last sip of beer, Aidan paid his bill and walked outside into the night. The feel of cold, Cascade Mountain air rushing through the ponderosa pines reminded him that winter would soon be upon the high desert. His favorite time of year.

"Ade," Briggs shouted, coming outside and breaking Aidan's reverie. "Look, I'm sorry I didn't say anything inside, but there is something going on—something big involving a lot of people—that's going to blow up this fucking town. I can't really tell you anything else, not even on deep background. But trust me, once shit goes down you'll be the first to know."

———————

As soon as Aidan got home, his five-year-old daughter Indie ran up to him and threw her little arms around his legs.

"Daddy, look what Mommy got me," she squealed, holding up a pink stuffed rabbit. "Isn't she cute?"

Aidan picked up Indie and then kissed his wife. Reina looked almost identical to their daughter. Both had deep brown eyes, short black hair and olive skin.

"What do you need help with, babe?" he asked, walking into the kitchen.

"Did you get the wine?"

Aidan pulled out a bottle of Reina's favorite Pinot Noir from a brown bag. Then he tried sneaking a taste of the vegetarian minestrone soup simmering on the stove.

"Get away from there," Reina said as she slapped his hand. "They should be here in half an hour. Can you set the table?"

Aidan saw Reina smile as he meticulously arranged those wine glasses on their oak dining set. The two continued preparing dinner together and chatting about their days at work until a knock on the door signaled the arrival of Cal and Jess Townsend.

"I'll get it," Indie said, racing to the door.

She let in their two friends who could not have looked more unlike one another. Jess always dressed up, preferring high heels with jeans that conformed to her body like a manikin.

Cal, on the other hand, grabbed whatever he could find in his closet. That meant he usually ended up wearing miss-matched socks and baggy T-shirts that never quite tucked into his cargo pants. And that was Cal dressed up. Aidan had unfortunately been to their house one too many times on the weekend to see his friend sporting slippers, white long johns and a hideous fur coat.

"Been a while," Aidan said as Indie grabbed their guests' hands and led them into the kitchen. "Babe, do you mind if I give Cal his gift while you girls finish getting ready?"

Cal's overgrown eyebrows wrinkled in surprise.

"Yeah, just don't take too long," Reina said as she hugged Jess.

Cal handed Aidan his fur coat as the two friends walked down to the basement.

"Where'd you get this piece of shit?" Aidan asked.

"Goodwill," Cal said. "Got a problem with that?"

Aidan entered the damp, half-finished basement that still reeked of mold from some dark and forgotten corner. Beside piles of boxes lay something hidden beneath a grey sheet.

"What is it?" Cal asked.

"Think of something you need."

"New coat?"

"Well, yeah, but I'm not buying you a coat."

Cal shrugged. Aidan ripped off the sheet, revealing a black Cannondale mountain bike.

"Oh my God," Cal said, caressing the lightweight frame with his heavy hands. "Ade, why'd you–"

"Because it's embarrassing riding with someone who uses a cheap-ass bike from Wal-Mart," Aidan interrupted. "Plus, we're both turning forty soon, so call it an early birthday present."

Cal wrapped his big arms around Aidan until he felt like he was going to burst.

"That's enough," Aidan said. "Just promise me you'll trash that other bike."

"Done. When we riding again?"

Aidan felt his cell phone vibrating in his pocket. "Great," he mumbled. "It's Mitch."

"I don't know if there's anything to this yet," his editor said. "But I just heard that the school board is holding a last-minute executive session Monday night. All the reporters are slammed, so I need you and Cal to come in early Monday and find out whatever you can ahead of time. Normally, I wouldn't give a shit. But why would they have this meeting closed to the public?"

Aidan thought for a moment. "Maybe the board members all bought Armani suits."

"I'm serious, Ade. This could be..."

"A front-page story," Aidan replied. "I know. Just like the Pet Parade. I'll talk to you Monday."

CHAPTER 3

On Monday morning, the girls begged their mom to let them call in sick for school.

They still felt exhausted from the party, but Ella refused. Said it would teach them a lesson about drinking too much. As their mom drove them to South County High, Zoey tried hiding deeper in her hood, but the car backfired. Ella swerved up to the main entrance. The girls lurched out of the car in embarrassment.

Like the last two years, Zoey moved down the halls with her head hung to the ground and her torn backpack slung over her right shoulder. She hoped nobody said hi. Nobody did.

Suddenly, she felt her phone buzz with another text. It was from *him*:

Look @ u2 lesbians.

This photo showed Zoey on top of Camille, their bodies entwined. Zoey shuddered, but the next text made her hair crawl:

Want me 2 delete these pics? Ull have 2 earn them. Ill tell you how soon. Im a patient and caring man, but if u don't obey, Ill send these to everyone @ school.

Another photo came through. A Snapchat. It showed a serrated hunting knife cutting into someone's back.

Zoey looked down the halls, wondering if the person texting was watching her. Maybe there was more than one. Maybe everybody at school was looking at nude photos of her right now. She could feel the blood draining from her cheeks.

Right as the picture disappeared, she saw Leah walk past her toward the lockers. That's when Zoey noticed something odd. Leah looked sick. Her usually perfectly straight hair was disheveled. Even more disturbing, Zoey saw the skin beneath Leah's right eye. Hidden beneath a mound of makeup appeared a dark shade of blue. Purple. Black.

"You OK?" Zoey asked.

Leah's eyes darted around the hall. "What do you want?"

"Something happened at your party," Zoey said.

Whatever color Leah had in her face faded completely.

"Sorry," the girl said, backing up and looking over her shoulder at something. Or someone. "I can't help you or Camille. I didn't mean for any of this to happen, but I can't do anything. It's too late."

When Zoey heard her sister's name, she realized that Camille had wandered away from her again. A feeling of concern crept inside Zoey as she searched for her sister. After a minute or two, she found her chatting with a group of girls. Like always, Camille was talking about Disney princesses.

"Who's your favorite princess?" Camille asked the girls. "Camille likes all of them, but her favorite is Snow White. She's called that because her skin is white as snow."

"Aren't you a little too old for that?" someone asked. "Where you from anyway?"

Zoey saw Camille's eyes twitch. Usually meant she was lying.

"Camille's from...Ohio. She loves all the mountains there."

The girls snickered.

"Do you always lie this bad and call yourself Camille?" another girl asked. "You some kind of retard?"

It was the first time Zoey heard this girl speak. Zoey decided she was a bitch.

Tears started to fall from Camille's childlike face as she slid bulky glasses over her amber eyes. Zoey thought they were beautiful. At least Zoey thought they looked better than her own green eyes, which resembled the color of seaweed.

"Let's go, Camille," Zoey said before her sister could answer. "Don't waste your time with these bitches."

The hall became silent. It almost seemed to darken, too, but that could have just been the clouds and snow shifting outside. Out of the corner of her eye, Zoey saw a boy smiling at her. He was cute.

"What'd you say?" the bitch asked. She got so close Zoey could smell her cheap perfume.

Thankfully, the bell rang. Zoey grabbed Camille's hand, walked her to class and then went to her own room for first period. Normally, she liked to sit in the back. But the entire row was taken by those same girls from the hall and apparently their boyfriends, or at least make-out partners.

"Sick," Zoey said as she watched "the bitch" snake her tongue inside a boy's mouth.

"Does your sister want some of this?" the girl asked. "Well, she'll never get any because she's probably never even kissed a guy—that fucking retard."

Everyone in the class laughed. Everyone except for that cute boy she saw in the hall.

"At least my sister hasn't fucked all the guys here," Zoey shot back, slinking into a seat in the middle.

The bitch stomped toward her. Just then, the door opened and their teacher stepped inside. The girl glared at Zoey before marching back to her seat.

"All right class, settle down," Mr. Brookstone said. "Now, one of the books we'll be reading this year is *David Copperfield*. Have any of you heard about this novel before?"

A few people nodded, but nobody talked.

"All right, who can tell me about the plot?" their teacher continued. "Why did David Copperfield have to work in the sweatshop?"

Zoey hated speaking up in any period, but she loved reading, and that book was one of her favorites. Zoey cherished every chance to forget her own bleak life and live in the world of another. It helped her forget her own problems—at least until the last page. Finally, she decided to raise her hand.

"Yes, Zoey," Mr. Brookstone said.

"Because his stepdad forced him to work there."

"Good, and why couldn't David just leave right away? Why'd he stay there?"

Zoey thought for a moment.

"Cause he was afraid of his stepdad. He was afraid of getting beat again."

Mr. Brookstone scribbled the word "Slavery" on the whiteboard.

"You hear that, class?" he said. "Zoey got to the heart of this story. Now, I know we don't have time to read a lot of books, so we're just going to be looking at a few chapters from several different novels that touch on this theme. While we do, I want you to be thinking about how slavery still affects people today and what we can do about it as a class project."

A girl raised her hand.

"I don't understand," she said. "Isn't slavery really different today?"

Mr. Brookstone took off his glasses and stroked his pointy goatee. "We've made some good progress, sure. But some things haven't changed much. People today are still forced into slavery. It may look a little different, but it's still the same crime."

People shifted uncomfortably in their seats.

"But not here in America," the girl said.

"You'd be surprised," Mr. Brookstone replied. "Now, we're going to be reading about some dark subjects this winter, but I want you to listen to this quote from Dickens in *David Copperfield*:

"I hope that simple love and truth will be strong in the end. I hope that real love and truth are stronger in the end than any evil or misfortune in the world."

Someone in the back farted. The class erupted as Mr. Brookstone tried to restore order.

For the next few periods, Zoey tuned out the world around her.

In each class, she could think of nothing but those photos. Those fucking photos. Nothing else made sense. Mathematic letters and numbers on whiteboards seemed to form some alien-like language.

When the last bell rang, Zoey couldn't wait to get home. She didn't want to see the bitch again, so she snatched her backpack, found Camille and headed toward the exit. Camille grabbed her hand. As usual, it felt rough and chapped.

Zoey thought about telling Camille she received another text and picture, but decided not to worry her even more. So Zoey just curled her lips, the best she could muster for a smile ever since That Night with her father. Zoey started to text her mom to see where she was, but Camille stopped her.

"Can we go to the rec center?" her sister asked. "Camille can't stop thinking about those pictures. She needs to get her mind off them or she'll go crazy."

Zoey didn't feel like hanging out with anybody, and she definitely didn't want to go to some lame rec center. But Camille looked so sad and scared.

"All right," Zoey said. "We can go."

Camille grabbed Zoey's hand and dragged her to The La Pine Recreation Center. Aside from the local Dairy Queen, every teen knew this building was the only other place to hang out in town, unless they wanted to drive to Bend, about thirty minutes north.

There was also the local library, but only nerds spent time there. Not the cool kids. Zoey didn't know which one she was. Frankly, she didn't give a shit. As they walked across the street, she tightened her hoodie and zipped it all the way up to her throat to keep the Cascade winds from cutting through her clothes.

"Do you remember it ever being this cold here?" Zoey asked her sister, who started skipping a little.

"Maybe," Camille said. "Other times it's really hot. Some days Camille thinks the weather's crazy, like her."

"I told you to stop saying that," Zoey replied.

Camille stopped skipping and started crying. "But everyone else seems to think so. Nobody else hates loud fire trucks and bright lamps and things that spin. Why don't you think Camille's crazy?"

Zoey faced her sister and wiped a cold tear from her face. "Cause crazy people don't ace all their math tests in junior high. And besides, everyone's a little crazy—even me. So stop caring about what other girls think of you."

Camille giggled as they walked into the rec center, where teens played games while others did their homework with after-school tutors. Camille squeezed Zoey's hand so hard it hurt.

"We need to go," her sister said.

"What's wrong?" Zoey asked.

"He's here. Oh God, he's here. That's the man who touched Camille."

Zoey had never seen someone look so scared. All of the color in Camille's face drained to ash white as she grabbed Zoey's hand and tugged her out the door.

"Who touched you?"

Camille didn't respond.

"Come on, you can tell me."

Her sister just stood there, shaking like a cornered animal. She flapped her hands again, rocking back and forth.

"It's OK Camille, you're OK," her sister said. "It's OK Camille, you're OK."

Zoey held Camille's head in her hands. Then she texted her mom to pick them up from the library. They walked across the street to the old building and waited inside. This was definitely the nerd hangout of La Pine. Here, scrawny boys played old computer games while gothic girls who looked like the girl with the dragon tattoo scoffed at models in magazines.

Zoey didn't know why, but she had a soft spot for the nerds. Maybe because they were shy and reclusive. Like her. Or maybe because they didn't give a damn what other people thought about them.

The girls sat in the back of the library with two cans of root beer. Camille finally started to calm down.

"So, who is he?" Zoey tried again.

"Camille's boss."

"You mean at your new county workshop?"

Zoey saw a slight spasm in her eyes.

"No, at Starbucks. Camille got another job in Bend. She's the manager there."

Zoey raised her right eyebrow at the lie.

Camille sighed. "Yeah, at the workshop. It's where we all work."

"What do you mean by 'we?'" Zoey asked.

Camille seemed annoyed. "The retards, of course."

Zoey hated it when her sister used that word. "Camille, how many times do I have to tell you to stop talking like that? You're not a..."

"Say it," Camille said, standing up. "Just say it—once and for all."

She glared at Zoey, testing her. The sound of computer

games grew louder. Her phone buzzed with a message that their mom was waiting outside.

"No," Zoey said. "Cause you're not. You're one of the smartest girls I know. Now, what do you mean he touched you?"

For a long time, Camille stared at the ground. Then she looked up at Zoey. "He touched my privates."

Zoey winced. "Did you tell anyone?"

"Yeah, but nobody did anything. Nobody ever does anything. Cause nobody believes Camille."

Zoey looked her sister straight in the eye. "Camille, are you telling me the truth? Yes or no."

By the strain on her sister's face, Zoey could tell she was trying hard not to twitch. But finally her eyes revealed the lie. Camille sat back down. She took another sip of root beer. And then she stared out the window at the falling snow.

"Camille's sorry," her sister said. "He didn't touch us, but he's always looking weird at the girls. Plus he's mean. He teases us. Nobody trusts him."

Zoey shook her head. "Camille, you've got to stop lying like that. One day something bad could really happen—and nobody will believe you. Do you understand?"

Camille didn't answer.

CHAPTER 4

On Monday morning, Aidan woke early to the alarm on his cell phone.

He sat up groggily in bed and glanced at the time. Six in the morning. Aidan tried getting up. But when he saw his wife lying naked next to him, he hit the snooze button and fell back to sleep. After another ten minutes, he woke a second time to the alarm.

"Damn it," Aidan said, striking the snooze button again. He caressed Reina's back for a few minutes like he always did, while thinking about what his editor had asked him to cover. He was still skeptical of the school board meeting, but knew Mitch would want a boring photo regardless. Aidan started to get up. Reina grabbed him by the arm and yanked him back to bed.

"Not yet," she said. "Just a few more minutes."

"Babe, I've got to go. I'll be late."

"No you won't."

Reina slid on top of him, kissed his mouth and pressed her warm chest against his.

"I'll try to be home early tonight," Aidan said. "How about we have dinner with your family and leave Indie with your parents for the night. Then we can get a couple drinks and...you know."

"Just don't stay too late."

"Don't worry."

Energized at the thought of an evening with his wife, Aidan took a shower, trimmed his beard, cleaned his glasses, grabbed his bag and then drove to work. He strutted through the tall wooden arches of The Times and waved to the receptionist while walking up the long stairs to the newsroom.

As soon as Aidan stepped inside, he saw Mitch bumbling toward him from the coffee pots. His mustache seemed particularly prickly and grotesque this morning.

"I'm about to go into our editors' meeting," Mitch said as his whiskers poked in and out of his mouth. "You'd better have some calls out by the time we're done. I want to know why the hell those fuckers at the school district are having another private meeting tonight."

Aidan sank into his chair. As usual, he hung up his jacket, rolled up his sleeves, arranged his pen and then placed his satchel in the right spot. Some mornings, like these, he just stared at the ink and coffee stains on that faded leather.

Reina had given him the bag as a gift when he got his first real reporting job at The Times. Back then he had been so proud. He was going to change the world with his photos. Give a voice to the voiceless. Comfort the afflicted. Afflict the comfortable. And do whatever other bullshit that journalism school had spoon fed him. But now, more than a decade later, that bag just reminded him how he was stuck in the same job. With the same old stories. And almost the same amount of debt from grad school.

"It's still a man purse, bro," someone whispered behind him.

"Go to hell, Cal. You wouldn't understand."

"Seriously, what do you keep in that bag?" Cal asked.

"Just some books, cigarettes, a couple tape recorders—you know, the basics."

Aidan plopped a piece of gum in his mouth and thumbed through his cell phone contacts to call the school board members.

"We still going to the meeting?" Cal asked.

"Yeah, it starts at four thirty," Aidan said. "But I'm hoping we can leave after an hour. I have a date with Reina tonight, so let's just take two cars. Plus, Mitch still wants me to get the latest school records ahead of time."

"Sounds like he's still got you doing two jobs."

"More like three. I'd better be getting a raise this year."

"You and me both, bro."

Aidan hopped into his Subaru and headed to the Mid-Oregon Schools District Office.

It was located on Wall Street, one of two main roads in downtown Bend. Seattle, on the other hand, had too many streets to count. He used to love getting lost in that city during college, blurring into the masses. No matter where he ended up, Aidan knew he could always find a place to get a good cup of coffee.

In Bend, there was only one good coffee shop: Strictly Organic. It was near the Old Mill District, where he saw a few brave souls still kayaking down the Deschutes River while he was pulling into the café parking lot. Normally he came here before covering a meeting. He needed the caffeine to keep him awake, and they served the best brew in town. It wasn't anything like Seattle, but at least they knew how to do a proper pour over.

Aidan ordered a cup. It was dark. Gritty. Just how he liked it. Then he sat outside and lit a cigarette. While inhaling the hot smoke and liquid, Aidan looked at the people around him. Mostly students and ski bums. Smoking e-cigs. Eyes glued to their cell phones. Ears attached to their headphones. And fingers stuck to their laptops, probably updating Facebook or Twitter. Nobody talked. So typical. And so fake.

Aidan couldn't help but notice how different the 80,000 people who lived in Bend were from the 1,000 or so who lived only thirty minutes south in La Pine. Both were part of Central Oregon's high desert, a rural region about 4,000 feet above sea level with a unique blend of volcanic buttes, ponderosa pines and black sagebrush. But that's where the similarities ended.

In the wealthy ski resort town of Bend, ladies shopped at boutique stores to spend their husbands' money on another piece of art or reclaimed wood to hang above their fireplace.

But in the rural region of La Pine, women split old wood in the forest to help their husbands heat the woodstove in their run-down cabin or trailer. During his reporting at The Times, Aidan had covered both cities, and he preferred La Pine. The people there felt more authentic—even if they did have a problem with drugs and crime.

After one last sip of coffee, Aidan drove to the school district office. He got the records half an hour later and began searching through them. For the third year in a row, both grades and attendance had increased. Although that didn't necessarily surprise Aidan, what piqued his curiosity was the fact that the greatest improvements came from schools in La Pine, where people earned about half the amount of money per year as those in Bend.

He spent a few more hours researching records and talking to staff at the office. Then Aidan remembered the meeting. He photocopied the records and raced to the boardroom. Out of breath, he motioned to Cal as they walked into the room and then sat in the back. Within the first few minutes, Aidan started to tune out as the superintendent, the school board members and the records administrator—Walter Mortenson—discussed the latest data and how that would probably improve their standing on the state's report card.

By six o'clock, Aidan started to get nervous. He had promised Reina he would be home early for a change, but the board members still had four more topics to address before moving into executive session. Aidan texted his wife:

Still in mtg.

She didn't respond. Finally, at about seven thirty, the board members got to the topic Mitch cared so much about.

"At this point, we're going to adjourn our main meeting and move into executive session," the superintendent said. "That means everybody except for the news media needs to leave now."

The few parents who had shown up to the meeting walked out, leaving Aidan and Cal alone with some of their least favorite people in the world.

"You guys staying?" the superintendent asked them. "Remember, you can attend this session, but you can't report anything from it according to–"

"We know the law," Aidan said. "How long you guys going to be?"

The superintendent just rolled his eyes, and the board members continued their meeting. At first, Board Member Devin Jameson talked in vague terms about the district's expenses. One of the members interrupted, asking why they had to discuss this in a meeting closed to the general public.

"Well, someone in Finance alerted me to some strange charges," Jameson replied.

"What kind of charges?" someone asked.

Jameson hesitated, glancing at the two journalists.

"Oh come on, just say it," another replied. "Those two can't report anything from this meeting anyway."

"One of these charges was at Jugs," Jameson said. "Someone spent school money there."

For the first time in years, Aidan felt that sickening urge again. It came out of nowhere and blindsided him, making his stomach churn. Old photos started flooding his mind, but he forced himself to pay attention to the meeting again. The board members were now talking about Gabriel Lester, who owned Jugs—La Pine's only strip club on the outskirts of town.

Surprisingly, Gabriel was considered a pillar of the community because he donated thousands of dollars each year to local charities. Aidan had tried covering the dark and grimy bar before, but without success. Nobody had returned his calls, and the few elderly residents who opposed it didn't want their names in the paper.

"How much money are we talking?" someone asked.

"More than five hundred dollars."

"What the hell?"

"Who did it?"

At first nobody answered. People shifted nervously in their seats. Then Jameson spoke.

"It's Walter's card."

Everyone stared at the records administrator, who worked full time for the district. Nobody talked. Aidan's heart beat fast. He could feel his head pounding as he watched Walter twitch in his seat, twirl his wispy hair and bite his disturbingly long fingernails.

"What the hell were you doing there during the day?" a board member asked.

"Why'd you use the district's card?" another said.

"Look, the card was a mistake," Walter replied, drumming his fingernails on the table. "I didn't mean to use it. Must've accidentally grabbed it from my wallet, instead of my own."

"Were you drinking?" another asked.

Walter stared at the table, boring his eyes into a brown spot where coffee had once been spilled. Then he got up and left the room. The board members adjourned the meeting. Aidan shot a few photos as Cal raced up to them, peppering the school leaders with questions. Everyone declined to comment. They tried finding Walter, but he had already left. So Aidan and Cal decided to drive to the strip club for answers.

He called Reina on the way. "Hey babe, it's me. Sorry the meeting ran late. But look, I've got to go cover something. Can we just reschedule for tomorrow night? Babe? You there?"

There was a long pause before Reina answered. "I thought you said this was going to change. No more late nights or not knowing what your schedule is. I thought you were going to stand up to Mitch."

Aidan's phone vibrated. He guessed Mitch was calling him.

"Rein, I'm sorry, but I've got to go. I'll give you a call when I'm on my way home."

———

A throbbing beat greeted Aidan and Cal as they pulled into the parking lot of Jugs.

Pulsating music escaped through a black door each time it opened for drunken men who stumbled out of the strip club and into the night. Aidan started walking toward the door, but realized that Cal remained back at his own car.

"You coming?" Aidan asked.

Cal shook his head.

"What the hell's wrong with you? Please don't tell me you've never been to a strip club before."

"No, I have. I just don't ever want to go back."

"Why?" Aidan asked. "They're not all that bad. It's just harmless fun. Plus, this is for work anyway."

Cal didn't budge.

"Fine, go home. I just want to see if I can get a few answers from some of these strippers."

A bouncer stopped Aidan once he got to the door.

"ID," the man said.

"What?" Aidan asked.

"You heard me. Show me your ID."

Aidan handed the bouncer his driver's license and paid the cover charge. The sickly smell of smoke, cheap liquor and body odor smothered him as he entered the club.

When he saw a topless woman start walking toward him,

that sickening urge returned again. All of a sudden, hundreds of old pornographic photos he had looked at in college came rushing into his mind, flooding it with bare flesh. Another young woman with big breasts and thick makeup walked right up to him.

"What do you want?" she asked, winking at him.

"Um, could I just get a glass of water?"

The stripper scowled at him. "I'm not a waitress, you prick."

Aidan felt out of place. Suddenly, he knew he shouldn't have come.

"Hey bitch, over here," Aidan heard a young man in front of him say to the main dancer on stage. This meathead must have been barely out of college. Based on the stupid hats he and his friends were wearing, Aidan guessed this was a bachelor party.

"Yeah, this bitch can move," the future groom said to the stripper. The dancer fondled her own nipples as she slid up and down a cold metal pole like she was riding the guy's shaft.

Another woman walked up to Aidan.

"What do you want?" she asked.

Unlike the last stripper, this woman looked normal. She wore little makeup. But what caught Aidan's attention the most were her eyes. Judging from the dark lines beneath them, she hadn't slept in a while. Overall, this woman just didn't seem to give a shit about her job—which meant she was the perfect target for his questions.

"How much for a lap dance?" Aidan asked. "Sorry, been a while."

"That's OK," the woman said.

Her mouth reeked of tobacco. Aidan guessed it was chew, based on the yellow tint to her teeth. The woman started to straddle his legs and touch his chest, but she kept yawning.

"I'm so sorry," she said, reaching her hands down toward his crotch.

"Don't worry about it," he replied. "Actually, I had a question for you."

"A question?"

"Yeah, and I'd like to just keep this between you and me if that's fine. I think there may be something going on between your boss and someone who works for the schools. Know anything about that?"

The woman jolted up from his chair and backed away.

"What the fuck?" she asked. "Are you a cop or something?"

Aidan glanced nervously around the room.

"Please be quiet," he said in a whisper. "No, I'm not a cop. I'm a news photographer. And I'm just trying to find out what's going on here."

The woman stormed away. Aidan put a few bucks on the table and walked back outside into the cold. He felt stupid. Once Aidan was about halfway to the car, he heard someone behind him.

"I'm sorry," the woman said. "It wasn't safe for me to talk to you in there. You're right. Something is going on here. I don't know what this school guy looks like or anything, but I can tell you I've seen a lot of really young girls hanging out around here during the day. I've even seen some leave with guys and walk across the street to the motel. Something's not right."

The woman kept looking behind her.

"Do you know any of these girls' names?" Aidan asked.

"I don't think so," she said. "Look, I can't talk anymore. I've got to get back on stage."

Aidan handed her a business card with his number.

"You can trust me," he said. "I'll come back again soon. By the way, what's your name?"

"Ella," she said. "Ella James."

As Aidan drove home from the strip club, he decided to celebrate by rolling the windows down and lighting a cigarette while a few snowflakes whipped through his hair.

He had that feeling in his gut. It was the sensation that only journalists knew. He had no clue where this story would lead, but he knew one thing—he was on to something. And it was good.

Aidan also knew he was in deep shit. He had promised to take Reina on a date tonight. So when Aidan finally got home, he started tiptoeing upstairs to apologize to his wife.

"What happened?" Reina asked from the living room.

"Oh shit," he said. "Babe, you scared me."

"I scared you? Ade, I've been up all night worrying about you. What happened?"

Aidan dropped his satchel on the ground and sat down next to Reina on their couch in the darkness. He could still smell the perfume she had put on for their date. It always reminded him of fresh flowers from the Saturday market. That made him feel even guiltier.

"I'm sorry," he said, flipping on a lamp. "I should've come home sooner. It's just, I got a great tip tonight. I don't know for sure, but it sounds like there's something real shady going on at the strip club—something involving high school girls. Look, babe, I'm so sorry about tonight. I really am."

"Stop," Reina said gently. "Honey, it's fine. I forgive you.

You've had a long night. I'm just glad you're OK. But please, promise me you'll be safe and let me know if you're going to be working late."

"I promise," he said, staring into her beautiful brown eyes. "Look, how about we get some sleep, and tomorrow I'll make it up to you? Hell, I'll even take you dancing this weekend like you've been wanting."

"I don't know," Reina said. "The last time we did that, you stepped all over my feet."

His wife put her legs across his on the couch. "Speaking of feet, can you please massage them? It's the least you can do to make up for bailing on our date."

Aidan smiled. "I knew that was coming. Good guilt trip."

CHAPTER 5

The next morning, Zoey made sure her mom dropped them off in the back.

But that didn't stop Zoey from running into "the bitch" a second time after she walked Camille to her class.

"Where's your little retard sister?" the girl asked as she slammed a locker shut right next to Zoey's face.

Zoey wanted to slam the girl's face into that locker, but she figured it would be a bad idea to get in trouble so early in the year. Plus, that school cop was roaming the halls nearby. Before Zoey could respond, the bell rang.

She zoned out for the next few periods. Then lunchtime came. Zoey hated lunchtime. Where you sat fixed your status. Picking one stupid table forced you to become a prep. Jock. Geek. Hipster. Or some sort of weird hybrid. Like last year, Zoey sat at a table by herself. She knew that made her a loner, practically a death sentence among most high school students. But Zoey didn't care. She preferred to eat her peanut butter sandwich by herself; the food pantry her mom went to rarely had jelly.

While eating lunch, Zoey checked her texts. Thank God, there were none from *him*. But there was a text from her dad that made no sense because it was filled with random letters and numbers.

Bastard, Zoey thought.

"Can I join you?" someone asked.

She looked up to see Josiah grinning at her. Aside from this childhood friend who grew up in trailer parks with her, Zoey didn't really know anybody else. Like her, Josiah didn't care where he sat. And like her, he also didn't give a damn about clothes. With his old work pants, flannel shirt and orange hunting cap, Josiah looked like he came to school straight off a farm. Zoey liked that. At least he didn't dress like most people at school with their white trash tank tops.

"Heard you got into a fight," Josiah said. "What happened?"

Zoey took another bite of her sandwich. "Someone called Camille a retard, Jo. So I called that girl a bitch. If that gets me on her bad side, I'd do it all over again."

"That's what I love about you," Josiah said. "You're always looking out for Camille."

Josiah's ash grey eyes were pale, almost weak. His curly red hair looked like a rat's nest spilling out of his cap.

"It's nice to see someone finally stand up to that girl," he added. "Sometimes I wonder why nobody–"

The sound of skipping interrupted Josiah.

"Jo's here! Jo's here!"

Zoey barely had a chance to turn around before Camille

hugged Josiah so hard it looked like the freckles on his face would pop.

While Camille told him every detail of the latest Disney movie, Josiah kept looking over at Zoey and smiling at her. Once her sister finished talking, it looked like Josiah was about to ask Zoey something.

But the bell rang before he could speak.

After school, Zoey and Camille went outside to wait for their mom.

She wanted to avoid everybody. Zoey just felt like being alone, curling into a ball on the couch and falling asleep by the space heater as the snow continued to fall.

Right as her mom pulled up, Josiah stopped her.

"Want to grab some Blizzards?" he asked. "My mom can pick us up. There's been something I've been meaning to ask you."

Zoey felt too cold for ice cream, but she knew Josiah loved their Dairy Queen trips. So she waved bye to Camille and her mom, then started walking with her friend.

The two headed down Coach Road to First Street, where they joked about the fact that the city had recently installed its first traffic light ever. Then they trekked north for a few minutes along U.S. Highway 97, the main corridor that connects La Pine to the rest of Oregon. The two had walked this stretch dozens of times since they were kids, and each time they could hear their moms in the backs of their minds telling them to be careful of the cars zipping by.

Zoey felt soaked when they finally made it to Dairy Queen.

Her hoodie proved no match for the snow that seeped through to her wet hair. Josiah ordered the Midnight Truffle Blizzard for both of them. They had tried every flavor on the menu, but kept returning to this one. As they sat down in a seat by the window, Zoey took her first bite. Then another. And another.

"Still your favorite?" Josiah asked.

Zoey nodded. For a brief moment, she wanted to tell Josiah everything that had happened at the party.

But *he* had promised to hurt Camille if she snitched. Plus, *he* had evidence. She couldn't stand the thought of someone humiliating them by sharing those pictures with everyone at school. She needed to destroy those. She just didn't know how—or what this person meant by the phrase that disturbed her most of all:

Want me 2 delete these pics? Ull have 2 earn them. Ill tell you how soon.

Zoey trembled when she thought about what this man wanted her to do to "earn them," let alone how "soon" that would happen. A blackness began to spread deep into her bones.

Josiah snapped her back to reality. "What's wrong, Zoey? You look exhausted."

"I'm just not feeling that great," Zoey said. "So, what were you wanting to ask me earlier?"

She waited for him to answer, but Josiah just sat there. His face turned bright red and highlighted his brown freckles even more.

"Sorry," he said. "It's just, Dad's been getting worse these days, and I don't know what to do about it."

Zoey stared into Josiah's weak eyes that penetrated the

wildness of her own. Something was different about him this year.

"Our dad's been getting worse, too," Zoey said. "He keeps sending me these drunken texts after being out all night. Good thing is, we hardly see him around much anymore. Mom tries to make sure we're long gone at school before he gets his sorry ass home to grab some food or clothes after staying out all night. Always takes off again right after that."

Josiah stopped chewing his truffles and put his spoon down. "I'm really sorry, Zo. Is he still cooking crank?"

"Yeah, and I know that's why Mom can't pay to wash our clothes or buy enough food. Any money she makes Dad spends on meth. And I'm getting sick and tired of that food pantry."

Josiah laughed. "Me, too. Their bread tastes like shit."

Zoey tried to smile.

"Can you take me home now?" she asked. "I really need to get some sleep."

"If you don't mind walking," Josiah said. "I just remembered my parents' car isn't working again."

"That sounds familiar. Hey, at least our trailer parks are close to each other."

"Yeah, but you're in the nice one. Lava Butte Park sucks."

"Are you kidding me?" Zoey asked. "Whispering Pines is way worse."

They both took one last bite of ice cream and then started walking together again. It didn't take long for Zoey to wish that she had remained inside the heated Dairy Queen with Josiah. The snow was now falling like clumps of wet cotton. Only a few trucks drove by. Nobody else walked on the lonely road.

Then Zoey saw Leah. The girl was heading toward her with

her boyfriend, Blake Dumpk, and two other senior boys. Zoey and Josiah tried to walk around them, but Blake and his buddies formed a blockade, their baggy pants sagging below their waists.

"Don't you ever talk like that to my bitch again," Blake told Zoey.

"Excuse me?" Zoey asked.

"You heard me."

Leah tried stopping Blake, but he slapped her across the face. When Josiah tried to intervene, Blake punched Josiah and threw him to the asphalt. Blood seeped from his nose onto a patch of grey snow. Zoey couldn't believe what was happening. But she didn't have time to think about it because Blake also slapped her.

Zoey's face stung. "What the hell? We're just trying to go home."

"Bitch wants to go home," Blake said. "Are you going to ask your retarded sister for help?"

"What do you want?" Zoey asked.

"Nothing," Blake replied. "Other than to beat up a lesbo. That's what you are, right? I mean, none of the guys seem to notice you. Nobody does."

Zoey heard somebody come up behind her. She recognized him as the cute boy she saw in the hall the other day.

"What the fuck is going on?" the boy asked.

"Damien, what're you doing here?" Blake replied. "You're not supposed to–"

"Shut up, Blake," Damien interrupted. "You'd better back off now before I fuck you up."

For a few seconds, nobody spoke. Then Josiah lunged again at Blake. He kicked him to the ground.

"You don't know how to fight worth shit," Blake said. "Let's see if your little friend knows how."

"Stop it, Blake," Leah said. "We don't need a fight."

Zoey remained in a state of shock. Blake tried hitting her again. But this time, Damien blocked it with his left forearm and shoved his right fist into Blake's jaw. As Blake collapsed to the ground, two other seniors rallied around him, trying to corner Damien.

Even though Damien was short, it seemed he knew how to fight. He kept his distance between the two seniors. One tried moving in on him from behind, but Zoey saw Damien bash the boy's left knee with his heel. The other senior threw a right punch. Damien blocked it with his left hand, put his other palm on the guy's shoulder, hooked his right leg behind his calf—and then slammed him to the cement. But as Damien backed up, Blake locked his thick arms around the boy's neck from behind. Choking him.

Zoey tried stopping them, but Blake just hurled her away. It looked like Damien couldn't breathe. His eyes closed. Head hung. Then Damien reached down and struck Blake in the crotch. The boy cursed, released his grip and crumpled to the ground. Damien kicked him hard in the head, and the senior passed out. The other boys ran away.

As Damien grabbed Zoey's hand, she shook from shock, still in disbelief over what had just happened.

"Are you guys OK?" Damien asked her and Josiah.

Zoey didn't say anything. She just stared into his bright blue, wolf-like eyes and at his rugged face with blond scruff.

"I'm Damien," he said. "Come on, it's freezing outside. The least I can do is take you guys home."

"I'll just walk," Josiah said, wiping blood from his nose.

"What?" Zoey asked. "You just got beat up. You shouldn't be walking home by yourself."

Zoey knew by the look on Josiah's emasculated face that she shouldn't have said that. "I'm sorry, Jo. That's not what I meant. You know it."

"No, you're right. I just got beat up. You should go home with someone who can protect you."

"Jo..."

He walked away. Slowly, Zoey got into Damien's car. It looked new. And smelled good. Like cedar wood. Zoey guessed that must have been his cologne. Judging from his nice jeans, silver chains and big rings, Zoey also figured that Damien didn't shop at thrift stores. But he made up for that with the fact that he was listening to Nine Inch Nails.

"I love this band," she said.

"Me, too. So, where do you need me to drop you off?"

"Whispering Pines," Zoey said. "Mom and I live there."

"The trailer park?"

Zoey felt embarrassed. Damien seemed to notice.

"Hey, I'm not judging you," he said. "That's the nice one from what I hear."

"You're not from around here, are you?" Zoey asked.

"No, I'm originally from Seattle. So, you sure you're OK? Blake didn't hurt you, did he?"

Zoey shook her head.

"Good. Make sure you stay far away from him and those girls—especially Leah."

"Why?" Zoey asked. "What's going on? I mean, Blake just tried to beat us up. He even hurt Leah, but she didn't seem to care or anything."

Damien's forehead twisted into a frown. "Just stay away from them, you hear?"

Zoey looked out the window.

"I'm sorry," Damien said. "I just don't want you to get... Just promise me you'll steer clear of them, OK? And by the way, I'm sorry I've never introduced myself before. It's my senior year, so sometimes I'm a little checked out."

The two continued talking until they pulled into The Whispering Pines RV Park, right off Highway 97. A mangy dog darted across the road. Probably looking in vain for scraps of food. Zoey apologized when they got to her lot. Damien stared at the old RV mounted on cinder blocks and plywood. Some empty beer cans littered the gravel next to the door, having spilled out of giant trash bags that were filled to the top with bottles. A bike without wheels leaned up against the cracked siding.

"It's got character," Damien said. "Can I come inside?"

"Um, no."

"Why not?"

"It's a hot mess."

Damien shrugged his shoulders. "I don't care."

Before Zoey could say no again, the door swung open as her mom stumbled outside wearing nothing but an old bathrobe. She had a can of Natty Light in one hand and a Lucky Strike cigarette in the other.

"Shit," Ella said. "I didn't know we were having company. Would've put something more proper on. Who the hell's this?"

"Well, you've met my mom," Zoey said as they got out of the car. "This is Damien, Mom. Please be nice to him."

Ella took a swig of her beer and sized Damien up.

"You're cute," she said. "What're you doing with my daughter?"

Damien chuckled as Zoey tried burying her face in her hoodie.

"Actually, I think she's pretty cute too," Damien replied. "Mind if we come inside? It's freezing out here."

Ella took one last chug of her beer and then opened the door for Damien and Zoey. The familiar hum of their space heater welcomed Zoey home, followed by the smell of rotten food. Her mom still hadn't cleaned up those damn dishes. Ella cleared a pile of dirty clothes from their couch, tossing it onto the ground.

"Sorry, haven't had guests over in a while."

Zoey's cheeks felt hot.

"Don't worry about it," Damien said as he sat down—and then shot right back up with a scream.

Zoey looked in horror at Quill, buried beneath the couch's arm. Quivering in defense, the ball-shaped creature bared its needle-like spines, ready to strike Damien again.

"What the hell is that thing?" he asked.

"Oh God, sorry Damien," Zoey said, now completely embarrassed. "That's Quill, my porcupine. I've been looking all over for her, but I guess I didn't search the couch."

To Zoey's surprise, Damien started laughing. "What kind of girl gets a porcupine for a pet?"

"What kind of guy wants to see a girl's trailer park?" Zoey replied with a smirk.

Suddenly, Damien stopped smiling.

"I'm sorry," he said as the color faded from his face. "It was nice to meet you, but I really need to get going now. I can't do this anymore. It's just not right."

CHAPTER 6

A idan got up before the sun.

He still felt guilty, so he decided to treat Reina to one of her favorite things—breakfast in bed. Despite his grogginess, Aidan grabbed a mixing bowl and started whisking together some flour, milk, sugar and real vanilla for the perfect pancake. He continued cooking until he heard some small feet pitter-pattering down the stairs.

"What are you making, Daddy?" Indie asked.

"Good morning, baby girl," Aidan said as he picked his daughter up and set her on a kitchen stool. "Why are you up so early?"

"I smelled cake," she said.

He laughed. Indie had called them that since she was a little girl.

"Want to help?" Aidan asked.

"Yeah," she said in a sleepy voice.

Aidan handed Indie a small cup that held the batter and helped her pour some onto the griddle. As usual, she made a mess. He always helped her form the liquid into some sort of animal that typically ended up looking more like a blob.

"Did you get hurt, Daddy?" Indie asked.

"What?"

"Mommy was scared for you. Did a bad guy hurt you?"

Aidan set the spatula down and stroked his daughter's hair. "No, you don't need to worry about your dad, OK? Everything's fine."

Indie's face wrinkled into a frown.

"But the bad guys won't hurt me or Mommy, right?" Indie asked.

"Of course not. I won't ever let that happen. I promise, OK?"

Before Indie could answer, the smoke alarm started blasting in their ears.

"Oh shit," Aidan said as he cranked open a window, fanned the alarm and threw a blackened pancake into the sink. Indie couldn't stop giggling.

"Don't you ever say that word," Aidan told his daughter. "Well, I bet your mom's awake now. Want to go bring her these other ones?"

"Shit, shit, shit," Indie said as she started carrying the pancakes upstairs.

"Indie, no. What did Daddy just say?"

"Daddy said shit."

Aidan chased his daughter up the stairs as Reina started coming down them.

"What's going on?" Reina asked, her eyes still half asleep.

"Indie, it's still dark out. What're you doing up so early?"

"Look Mommy, me and Daddy made you some breakfast."

"Oh, that's nice," Reina said as she kissed him. "Thanks, babe."

"Sorry about the alarm. I didn't mean to wake you up."

Aidan looked at Indie as she grinned back at him.

"All right, I need to get to work. I'll be back in time to help with dinner. I love you both."

After kissing his wife and daughter goodbye, Aidan poured some coffee into his travel mug and drove to work. At five in the morning, most of the city was still asleep. Only late-night drinkers and a few baristas were braving the icy roads.

Aidan loved early mornings. It was the time when the light was warmest and fell softly on his lens. He could capture that perfect shot of a red fox scurrying through the forest or the sun rising to illuminate the Three Sisters mountains. He had hiked the South Sister many times, photographing lizards darting among the white, gnarled trees and spotty shrubs by Devil's Lake Trailhead.

Aidan also loved the eerie silence that came from nobody else in the newsroom. He arranged his gear as usual and then started checking the wires to see if there were any late-breaking stories. Like most days, it was quiet.

That's when he heard the police scanner explode with chatter.

Between the cryptic codes he still didn't understand, Aidan could tell that sheriff's deputies had surrounded a motel in La Pine. Then the sound of gunfire tore through the speakers of the scanner and made him spill his coffee.

"Holy shit," Aidan said as he grabbed his satchel, bolted out the door and sped to La Pine. He got there within twenty minutes, a personal record, only to find a few deputies left at Motel

Thrift, located right across from Jugs strip club. He took a couple quick shots.

"I knew you'd be here," Deputy Briggs said.

"What the hell happened?" Aidan asked. "I heard gunshots. That true?"

"Yeah, we had a little confrontation, but nobody got hurt. Looks like you may finally have a real story. Don't worry, you'll get the report."

"Come on, man. Just tell me a little more. What happened here?"

Briggs rolled his eyes. "You're such a nosy bastard. We arrested someone who was with a young girl."

"Oh my God. How young?"

"That's enough, Ade. You'll see the report soon enough."

Aidan thought for a moment about his conversation with Ella at the strip club. "One more thing. What's the girl's name?"

Briggs shook his head. "You know I can't do that. She's a minor."

"Look, you know me," Aidan said. "We're not going to print anything. This is completely off the record."

The deputy leaned in close.

"Leah Colson," he whispered. "Now go fuck off. Don't you have a Pet Parade or something to cover?"

Aidan sped back to Bend. That feeling in his gut just grew stronger.

CHAPTER 7

During her first two years at South County High, Zoey had talked to almost nobody, aside from Josiah.

But this year, she had already managed to meet a bitch, a bully and a boy who got stabbed by her porcupine. She didn't think life could get any worse in La Pine.

Then Zoey saw her dad.

It was a late Saturday morning, and she awoke to the sound of crackling bacon. Zoey's mom almost never cooked, so she knew that bastard was in the kitchen.

"Dad, what're you doing?" Zoey asked.

"Morning," Ricky replied. "Made you some bacon. Extra crispy."

Zoey stared at her father's teeth. At least what was left of them. She had punched one out That Night, while the rest were rotting from too much meth. His face still looked skeletal, covered in sores and dark bags under his eyes.

"Come on," her dad said as he heaped a pile of deep fried strips onto a paper plate. "Mom said you still like your meat that way."

"Where's Mom?"

"I'm right here, honey," Ella said as she emerged from the bedroom with Camille. "Your dad came home late last night."

Zoey could tell her mom was scared. Terrified. She'd seen that look in her eyes before.

"I've sobered up," her dad said. "Not cooking anymore. I'm done with that shit. Now you all just sit down and eat some bacon with me like a good family."

Nobody sat down. Ricky slammed his fist on the table. "I told you all to sit down."

This time they obeyed. They sat in silence for a while. Normally, Zoey devoured bacon. But the sight of that pig grease oozing from her father's yellow teeth and dribbling onto his grey beard made her feel sick.

"What the hell's wrong with all of you?" her dad asked. "Why aren't you talking to me? I want to hear about what's been going on around here. How about you, Camille?"

Camille started to cry. Zoey held her sister's hand beneath the table.

"Ricky, please," her mom said. "Don't do this in front of the children."

"Do what?" he asked. "I just want us all to be one big happy family again."

Zoey couldn't take it anymore.

"You're too late for that," she said.

Her dad jumped up from the table.

"What the fuck does that mean?"

"Ricky, stop," Ella said. "Please, just leave the girls alone."

For a brief moment, Ricky raised his fist.

"Fine," he said and grabbed the rest of the bacon off of their plates. "That just leaves more for me then. Why don't you all go get dressed and I'll clean up in here."

Zoey dragged herself into their only bathroom and shut the door. She tossed off her shirt and sweatpants. Wearing only her small bra and panties, she stood shivering by the shower, waiting for it to heat up. Took forever in their trailer. Once the water finally felt warm, she started unhooking her bra but noticed that she hadn't closed the door all the way. She shut it again.

As always, Zoey took a long shower. It was her sanctuary—the only place she felt completely alone and at peace. She loved the feel of the hot water as it soothed her skin. Each drop seemed to take another worry from her mind as it trickled down her head. Over her body. Into the drain. After half an hour, Zoey dried off and applied some more black eyeliner, especially beneath her left lid.

That's when she noticed the bathroom door was still open.

"Seriously?" she said, slamming it hard this time. Zoey heard a dull snap, followed by what sounded like a curse. She froze. "Hello?"

Nobody answered, but Zoey knew it was her dad. He had been watching her. Staring at her. And she had just slammed the door on his fucking face. It had been more than a year since That Night, but all of those feelings came back with a sick feeling that started in her stomach and ended violently on the floor with a pool of vomit. Zoey shook. Her head spun. She collapsed to the ground.

When she awoke only a few minutes later on the couch, her

mom was holding her, crying. Zoey looked around the room, but that bastard wasn't here.

"Where is he?" Zoey asked.

"Out in the yard splitting some wood," Ella said. "What's going on?"

"It happened again, Mom."

Ella gasped right as Ricky came back inside.

"Get the fuck out," Ella said. "I'm divorcing your sorry ass once and for all. You stay away from my girls. You hear me?"

Ricky punched her in the face. "Don't tell me what to do, you little cunt."

Ella shrieked in pain as she shielded Zoey and Camille from her husband. But instead of beating the three of them, Ricky bolted out of the trailer. Zoey raced outside after him and tried cussing him out, but he just flipped her off and kept walking in the snow.

Once Zoey got back to their trailer, she spent the next few hours trying to calm Camille down while applying ice on her mom's bruised face. Finally, by late afternoon, Zoey decided she had to see Josiah. For some reason, she felt safest with him. At least he was safer than home. Zoey also thought about Damien, but she barely knew him, while Josiah could remember her Hello Kitty lunchbox from elementary school.

Zoey told them goodbye and walked to where she could always find Josiah: at the local feed store. As she entered the run-down shop off the highway, the smell of worms, guns and feed made Zoey feel like she had gone back in time one hundred years.

"Need something?" asked a gruff voice behind the counter.

The voice belonged to Josiah's dad, a slug of a man who must have weighed more than 400 pounds. His butt spilled over his stool, enveloping it in fat. He eyed Zoey with curiosity as his puffy white hands rose up and down atop his stomach that expanded like a balloon with each breath.

"Is Jo here today?" she asked.

The man cleared the phlegm from his throat and swallowed alive an entire cheese puff.

"What's it to you?" he asked.

"We're supposed to go over our homework together," she lied.

The man popped another cheese puff into his mouth and sneezed. A line of spit mixed with cheese crumbs dangled from his lips like a broken spider web. Then Marge walked behind the counter.

"Bill, you scaring off our customers again?" she asked. "Oh, hi Zoey. Sorry, Bill's a little consumed with his snacks. What do you need, dear?"

"Hey, Marge. I'm looking for Jo. Is he here?"

The woman's soft, gentle eyes brightened.

"Yeah, I'll go get him for you," she said, right as Josiah walked into the shop. "By the way, thanks for helping my son the other day. He told me about that bully. Jo's nose is still a little sore, but it's not too bad. I heard you and another boy saved him."

"That sounds about right," Bill said as he folded the string of spit back into his wet mouth. "That's our pussy of a son."

"Stop it, Bill," Marge said. "That's not what I meant. And you know it."

Zoey stared at Josiah. He looked defeated. So she decided to lie.

"Actually, Jo saved me. He took out one of the bigger boys who slapped me in the face."

"That's my boy," Marge said.

Marge patted Jo's back and then turned toward her. "Now Zoey, would you like some hot cocoa? I can make you some in our RV. We don't have any milk or marshmallows, but it'll warm you right up."

"Sure."

Zoey winked at Josiah as the two walked under darkening skies with his mom into their trailer parked behind the feed store. He grinned sheepishly. Zoey couldn't believe how much smaller Josiah's RV looked. She used to play in here with him as a kid, but Zoey couldn't remember the last time she had actually seen it. At least she and her mom had somewhat of a kitchen.

But their kitchen—if you could even call it that—shared space with the dining room and living room. She saw only one bed. Judging by the sleeping bag on their couch, Zoey guessed that was where Josiah slept. He looked embarrassed.

"I like what you've done with the place," Zoey said. "At least you've got a sleeping bag for your couch. I've just got a blanket."

That made him grin again.

"It's not much," Marge said. "But it's about all we can afford right now, what with the Recession and all. At least we can enjoy a good cup of cocoa every now and then."

Zoey watched as Marge poured a bag of powdered mix into a pot of boiling water. The smell made her think of Christmases long ago. Without warning, Zoey broke down.

"What's wrong, dear?" Marge asked.

"Nothing," Zoey said. "I'm sorry. I didn't mean to do that. I know it's been a while, but can I stay over here tonight? Things aren't really going well at home right now."

"Does your mom know you're here?" Marge asked.

Zoey nodded.

"I tell you what," Marge said, handing her the drink. "Why don't you text your mom to let her know you're OK and are staying with us. It'll be just like all those sleepovers when you were a little girl. I'll finish making you this cocoa, and then you can just go curl up on the couch like old times. Josiah can sleep outside tonight."

Zoey looked at Marge in shock.

"I'm just kidding, dear. We've got an extra cot."

Once Josiah's mom left, Zoey started telling him what had happened at home. But after a few sips of the hot cocoa, she fell asleep.

Zoey woke to the smell of cinnamon rolls.

She ate two of them with Marge and Josiah. Bill was still working at the shop, even though most people were at church or still sleeping. After downing another cup of cocoa, Zoey thanked them for breakfast.

"You're welcome, dear," Marge said. "Now, we'd better get you home so your mom doesn't worry."

When they arrived at the trailer, she saw her mom pacing outside and spitting tobacco-stained wads onto the dirt. Ella raced up to Zoey and hugged her.

"Oh God, I'm so sorry Zo," she said. "I should've never let your dad come back in like that. He just seemed so real this time, almost like he'd..."

Ella started crying. Zoey held her tight.

"It's OK, Mom," Zoey said. "Just please, promise me we won't ever see him again."

Ella nodded and then waved to Marge. "I'd offer you in for some supper, but I haven't been to the food pantry yet."

"Me neither," Marge said with a smile. "We should go shopping again together. Been too long. What're you doing tomorrow afternoon?"

The two women continued talking as Zoey and Josiah smiled at each other. The snow had finally stopped.

"Thanks for standing up for me to my dad last night," Josiah whispered.

"You earned it," Zoey said.

Once Jo and Marge left, Zoey talked to her mom for a while. Felt so good. She hadn't connected with her mom like that in such a long time. By then most of the eyeliner had bled down her cheeks, revealing her scar. But she didn't care. Not around her mom. Josiah was another story. Even though she knew him well, she still hadn't told him everything about her dad. What he had done to her.

Not yet. Not for a while.

———

The next day, Zoey and her sister returned to school.

But Zoey couldn't focus again. Any time she tried to concentrate on math, science or literature, her mind drifted to those photos. Several times she felt her leg vibrate with a text, but it was just her mind playing tricks on her.

Finally, the last bell rang. Zoey found Camille, who begged her to visit her new sheltered workshop through the county. Before Zoey could answer, Damien appeared.

"Hey girls," he said. "Zoey, can I talk to you for a sec?"

Zoey looked at Camille, who stepped aside.

"So, about the other day," Damien said, lowering his voice. "I shouldn't have just left like that."

"What happened?" Zoey asked.

"I can't talk about it right now. But I really was having a great time, OK?"

"I still don't understand," Zoey said. "Why'd you just leave like that?"

Damien gritted his teeth. "It's something to do with my dad. I just needed to get away, but it had nothing to do with you. Can you just trust me on that?"

Damien had already proved himself once by protecting her, so she nodded. Then she told him goodbye and headed to the workshop with Camille.

Zoey felt like she had wandered into another world. Inside the workshop, grown men and women sat in cell-like cubicles. Some drew pictures with crayons. Others played with dolls in the dull windowless room. The only rays came from above by fluorescent bulbs that needed to be changed a long time ago. To Zoey, this factory felt more like a mix between a nursery and a nursing home.

Those who weren't confined to cubes stood in a long row with other people who assembled mechanical parts. The pieces came to them from a black hole that spit each item onto an endless conveyer belt, which stretched like a tongue. The mouth never quit. Never stopped. Just kept spitting more and more parts onto the belt.

"What is this place?" Zoey asked.

"Camille already told you. It's the sheltered workshop."

"What are they sheltering you from?"

Camille thought about that for a moment. But then a man in front of them started screaming uncontrollably.

"Behavior problem in Cube Two," someone shouted over the intercom. A social worker raced toward the man.

"That's him," Camille said as she pointed to the social worker. "That's the boss we hate."

"Dustin, stop," the social worker said. "You know you're not supposed to do that."

Dustin kept screaming.

"Stop now or I'm going to restrain you," he repeated.

Dustin didn't care. He just kept screaming. The room became silent except for the never-ending hum of the belt. The social worker tried to control him, but Dustin spit on the man's shaved head. Zoey could see a deep blue vein bulging from his skull.

But instead of restraining Dustin, the social worker whispered something into his ear. Zoey had no clue what he said. But whatever it was, Dustin became terrified. He shook. Lurched back. And cowered outside his cube.

"I'm so sorry you had to see that," the social worker said as he walked up to them. "You must be Camille's sister. She's told me so much about you. My name's Jacob. I'm one of the supervisors here."

The man held out his hand, but Zoey didn't shake it.

"You should be proud of your sister by the way," Jacob said. "Camille just got a big raise. Finally made it to one dollar an hour, like Dustin."

Zoey looked at Camille, who tried to muster a smile.

"A dollar?" Zoey asked. "Are you kidding me? Isn't that illegal?"

"Of course not," Jacob said. "This is a sheltered workshop.

We don't have to pay minimum wage."

"Why?"

Jacob shrugged his shoulders.

"Who knows," he said. "Look, I don't make the rules. All I know is that people like Dustin and your sister can't assemble as many parts as a normal person, so it makes no sense to pay them the same. That's why the county's new partnership with the schools has been so great. Some of these kids would never make it in the real world."

Zoey wondered if that was really true—or just a bullshit excuse to keep their costs down.

"All right Camille, time to get to work," Jacob said. "You're already behind. It was nice to meet you, Zoey. Maybe we'll see each other more often."

As Camille got ready for work, Zoey wondered if Mr. Brookstone was right. Maybe some things still hadn't changed much since *David Copperfield*. At least David was able to get another job outside the sweatshop. But in or outside this workshop, Dustin and Camille were just two more bodies on an hourly assembly line. Worth one dollar each.

Right then, her phone buzzed with another text:

Still want pics? Meet me @ Motel Thrift @ midnight. If u don't, Jo will see u like this.

The message included another Snapchat photo of two bodies lying in a ditch by the side of a dirt road.

Zoey couldn't take it anymore. Every time her phone vibrated now, her whole body jerked, knowing it could be another message from *him*. She had to get rid of it. Of every chance for him to terrify her with another bruised, bloody or sickening photo. So she threw her phone on the ground. Zoey was about to smash it with her boot, but Camille stopped her.

"Another one?" her sister asked.

Zoey nodded. "Wants us to meet him tonight at a motel."

"What're we going to do?"

Zoey had no clue. She texted her mom to pick them up. Half an hour later, she still hadn't heard anything, so they decided to walk home.

Their mom wasn't around when the sisters got back to the trailer. Zoey and Camille threw their backpacks on the floor and sat on the couch. The sound of the clock above the sink grew louder. Zoey could feel every click pound in her chest. *Tick. Tock.* Another second closer to meeting him.

Him.

She didn't even know who *he* was. That was the scariest part. It had to be Blake or one of those other boys who tried beating her up the other day, but she wasn't sure. No proof. Maybe it was a kid from another school who came to the party. Maybe it was some creepy old pervert who snuck into the party. Either way, Zoey didn't want to meet *him* at some shady motel.

After several hours of trying to come up with a plan, Zoey gave up. She and Camille had come no closer to figuring out what they were going to do about tonight. As Camille put her head on Zoey's shoulder, she started to feel tired. Maybe this person was just joking. Maybe this was just some kind of sick prank. Maybe he would just go away. The two sisters fell asleep together on the couch.

The sound of pounding on the trailer door woke the girls up. Zoey looked at the clock. Eleven o'clock. *Tick tock. Pound. Pound. Pound.* Before she could do anything, her dad burst through the door.

"Hey girls," he said. "You're looking good tonight."

Zoey stepped back. "Where's Mom?"

Ella stumbled into the trailer, barely able to stand. Then she passed out on the floor.

"Your mom's fine," Ricky said. "Real fine. I gave her a good strong drink when we met to sign those fucking divorce papers. Should be out for a while, so I thought we could have a little daddy-daughter time—just like we used to."

Zoey could tell her father was undressing her with his eyes. She felt naked next to him, even with her hoodie.

"Want to take a shower with me?" he asked.

Zoey froze. He stepped closer. She could smell rum in his rotten teeth. Without warning, he touched her.

"You're so small, but so hot, Zoey. What do you say we go back to the shower? Camille can join us this time, too."

Zoey couldn't breathe. Couldn't think. With his hand still on her, Zoey walked backwards with slow steps, leading him right to her porcupine's cage. In the second that he closed his eyes to kiss her, Zoey grabbed Quill. Shoved the needles into her father's face. And kicked him with her steel-toed boots.

Then Zoey and Camille bolted out the door.

CHAPTER 8

Aidan still hadn't gotten a copy of the police report about that motel shooting.

From his experience, it could take a while to get public records from local government agencies. Officials seemed to love violating state records laws, probably because most papers didn't have the time—or the balls—to challenge them.

"Any news on that motel?" Mitch asked. "The TV stations are still saying everything from rape to murder."

"Not surprising," Aidan replied. "I won't know anything for sure until we get a copy of the damn report, but it sounds like they arrested someone for having sex with a minor."

"That fucker," Mitch muttered. "All right, forget about all other assignments today. I want you and Cal to focus only on this."

"You mean I don't get to cover the Sisters Quilt Show? I was looking forward to that."

"You'd better get working before I change my mind, you little prick."

Aidan laughed as he fired up his laptop and put his pen, notebook and satchel in their proper places. Despite his disagreements with Mitch, he had to give his editor credit. Whenever a big story broke, Mitch was willing to toss out everything else to get it right. Usually.

The rest of the morning, Aidan worked with Cal to gather as much information as they could while waiting for the police to release their facts. Finally, they came that afternoon:

Deputies arrested a Bend man on charges of unlawful sexual contact with a minor at a La Pine motel.

Aside from a few more details, that was it. Normally the reports were a little longer and more in-depth, but not this one. Aidan and Cal tried getting more information from the sheriff's office, but everyone declined to comment as the investigation was still ongoing.

"Son of a bitch," Mitch said as they gave him an update. "All right, here's what I want you guys to do. Cal, write what you know. Ade, go back to La Pine and take some more photos. Also, you said Briggs gave you the girl's name off the record, right? Well, find her. Maybe the cops already released her. I want copy and photos on my desk by four. Now go."

Aidan drove straight to Leah Colson's house, where some TV reporters were leaving and shaking their heads, wishing him better luck in trying to get an interview. Aidan knew he had one advantage over the TV stations; he could promise Leah complete anonymity because Mitch would never let him print the name of a minor anyway. So he rang the doorbell. Hoping for the best.

A woman opened the door a crack. "Are you another fucking reporter?"

"Yeah, but I have information that can help your daughter."

"Get the hell off our property."

The woman slammed the door. Aidan started walking back to his Subaru as the wind picked up again among the pine trees.

"Wait," the woman said, opening the door again. "My daughter wants to talk to you."

The woman led Aidan inside, where Leah was shaking on a couch. She had dark bruises under both of her eyes. Aidan sat down next to her and waited.

"If I talk, will you promise never to use my name?" the girl asked.

"Absolutely," Aidan replied. "My editor would never let me do that."

Leah looked skeptical. "I mean ever. Do you understand?"

Aidan nodded. The girl's mom started crying. Leah told her to leave the room and then looked at Aidan.

"Do you have a tape recorder?" she asked.

"Yeah, why?"

"Let me see it."

Aidan handed her one of the tape recorders from his bag. She took the batteries out and handed it back to him.

"You're the first person I'm telling this to," Leah said. "In fact, the only reason I'm talking to you is because I don't know what else to do. The other reporters were jerks. And those fucking cops all treated me like shit, even when they released me. But Mom just said you know something that can help me."

Aidan told the girl about his conversation with Ella and what he knew about a potential connection between the strip club owner and the school records administrator.

"I knew people were starting to notice," Leah said, shaking even harder. "Jesus, he'll kill me if he finds out I talked. The last time I tried, he gave me this."

Leah pointed to multiple bruises on her face.

"But you've got to know that someone blackmailed me," the girl continued. "Someone who works for the schools. I thought I loved him, so we had sex one time in the girl's locker room. But he recorded it and then threatened to show that video to my mom if I didn't fuck his friend."

Leah started sobbing. He couldn't help but stare at her bruises. Someone had hurt her. Bad.

"I thought that was it. But then I kept getting more messages, telling me to meet more of his friends. Sometimes we'd meet at that motel. Other times we'd do it in the back of a strip club. I wanted to tell Mom so bad, but they said they'd hurt me and my brother if I said anything."

Aidan looked at a family photo on the wall. Her brother couldn't have been much older than Indie.

"So I kept doing it," Leah said. "Sometimes I'd be out all night. Of course, my grades started to drop. But then, this guy was able to change my grades to make them look better. There was one month where I missed a lot of days, but he changed that too. Now I don't know how to get out of this shit. I think I wanted to get caught the other night."

Aidan couldn't believe what he was hearing.

"Did you tell the police this?" he asked.

"Weren't you listening? They said they'd hurt my little brother. He's only six."

Leah was now shaking so hard he thought she would go into a seizure any second.

"There's just one more thing you've got to know," she said. "I'm not the only one. There are some other girls I was forced to recruit. I'm supposed to invite them to parties. Slip some drugs in their drinks. Have a few boys take some pics while they're passed out—and then blackmail them."

Leah handed Aidan a sheet of paper with thirteen names scribbled on it and then buried her face in her hands.

"Those are the girls," she said. "Including the two newest recruits, Zoey and Camille. Oh God, I'm so sorry. I never meant to do this."

Aidan stared at the names in disbelief. "I don't understand. How was this guy at school just able to make your records look better all of a sudden?"

Leah shrugged.

"I don't know all the details," she said. "All I know is he's been taking our names out and then putting them back in to get rid of any bad grades or missed days. That's how I've been told to explain it to all of my recruits, anyway."

Aidan strode over to the girl and put his hand on her shoulder, but she recoiled like a snake and shoved him away.

"What do you want me to do?"

The girl thought for a moment and then took a deep breath. She looked up at him with eyes that seemed to burn with fire.

"I want you to take these assholes down," Leah said. "I don't know who all is involved in this gang or how far up this goes, but you can start with that records guy. He's the one who fucked me and forced me into this."

CHAPTER 9

Zoey rarely ran.

But this time, she and Camille raced as fast as their scrawny legs could move until they reached the main highway. And this time, the first person Zoey wanted to find was Damien. He had protected her once before. She needed his help again now more than ever. Zoey grabbed her cell and called Damien. No answer. She tried Jo. Voicemail.

Zoey and Camille kept running. Snow had already begun to fall on the lonely road, but Zoey was only wearing her blue jeans and black hoodie that she tightened over her head. The sound of snow crunching beneath Zoey's feet made her jump a few times and glance behind her into the darkness. Nothing. In fact, she only saw a few trucks pass by as they continued heading south. Zoey had no plan—other than to get the hell away from La Pine.

Maybe they'd hitchhike to Seattle. At least in that city Zoey guessed she could disappear into a crowd. She couldn't do that in La Pine. Even the trees felt like they were surrounding her. Suffocating her. Trapping her in this goddam town.

Finally, Zoey saw some warm lights ahead. They stumbled into Baldy's Truck Stop and sat in a booth by the back. Zoey ordered a hot chocolate and stared out the window at the snow that was now falling like heaping bags of powdered sugar. She ran her hands through her hair and started sobbing. So did Camille.

"Girls, you need help?" a waitress asked.

"No, we're fine," Zoey lied. "I just broke up with my boyfriend."

"Well, let me know if you need anything. We've got some nice hot waffles that'll warm you right up. It's on the house."

Zoey took another sip of cocoa and felt her phone vibrate. It was Damien. She asked him to meet them at the truck stop immediately.

Within minutes Damien arrived. He sat across from her and ordered a coffee. After a long sigh, Zoey explained everything. She told him about the shower. The groping. Her pet Quill. When she mentioned the porcupine, Damien couldn't help but laugh.

"I would've loved to see your dad's face," he said. "I don't know what's worse: getting beat up by your own daughter—or the fact that you used a porcupine."

Zoey tried to smile, but then she remembered the text. It told her to meet *him* at the motel around midnight—in ten more minutes.

"Can we stay at your parents' house tonight?" Zoey asked.

Damien looked away. "They're out of town this weekend."

"Please, we just need somewhere to stay. We can't go back home right now."

The waitress came back and handed Damien his coffee. She frowned at him.

"I have an idea," Damien said after the waitress left. "Do you and Camille want to take a road trip with me to Seattle? I know a small house we could rent for the weekend."

Zoey drummed her fingers on the table. The rhythm reminded her of that clock ticking in their trailer. Counting down. Nine minutes. Now eight.

"All right," Zoey said. "But only if we leave right now."

Damien paid for their drinks and then walked them out to his car. As they got in, Zoey could tell he was wearing that cologne again. God it smelled good. Suddenly, she felt hot and took off her hood.

"Your hair's pretty," Damien said as the girls hopped in his car. "I think this is the first time I've really seen it. You always cover it up."

Zoey turned her phone off. The three sat in silence as they headed north on Route 26 toward Mt. Hood through the Government Camp pass. While listening to Nine Inch Nails, Zoey stared out the window at the frozen mountains of the Cascades. They looked eerily white against the ink black sky. Zoey forgot how much she hated driving over mountain passes, especially at night. She tried not to glance over at the flimsy guardrail—the only thing that kept them from flying off the cliff.

Finally, Damien broke the silence. "So, why hasn't your mom divorced your dad? He sounds awful."

"Mom's tried to leave," Zoey said. "But each time Dad promises to change. And each time that asshole lies."

"I'm sorry," Damien said. "But I can understand. My mom did the same thing with my dad until she finally left town altogether. We haven't heard from her since. So, do you still talk to your dad at all?"

Damien looked over at Zoey, but she didn't answer.

"It's fine," he said. "Hey, I'm not going to tell anybody. Plus, we still have more than six hours to drive."

Zoey started to put her hood back over her head.

"You don't need to do that," Damien said.

"What?"

"You don't need to hide from me, OK? You can trust me."

Zoey took her sweatshirt off altogether, talked for a little bit more and then fell asleep for the rest of the trip.

The next morning, she awoke in a small room to the sound of seagulls.

Zoey had never heard their noisy squawk before because she'd never been outside Central Oregon, let alone in a big city like Seattle. Their call sounded almost peaceful, especially with a cool breeze blowing through the window. For a brief moment she panicked. But then Zoey saw Camille asleep on the couch across from her and Damien snoring on the floor.

She turned her phone back on. Almost noon. Her mom had left dozens of texts and voicemails, but there were none from *him*. Thank God. She wondered if it really was just a sick prank or some really bad dream. Zoey knew her mom would be worried about them, so she decided to tell her that they were staying at a "friend's house" for the weekend because they couldn't stand the thought of seeing Dad again right now. She left out the fact that they were in Seattle.

Zoey grabbed her hoodie and snuck outside. The smell of fresh air from Lake Union was so different than the rivers in

Bend. Some people jogged. Others rode bikes. But what struck Zoey the most was how many people there were. Some mornings in La Pine when their car wasn't working, she could count on one hand the number of people she saw while walking to school. Zoey took one last breath of fresh air and then stepped back inside the house.

She nudged Damien. "You just going to sleep all day or what?"

"Good morning to you too," he said.

The three got dressed and then took the bus to Pike Place Market. Zoey reveled in the smell of fresh salmon, roasted coffee and warm loaves of bread. They walked to the pier and found a diner where they ate a full meal of eggs, bacon, home fries and hot sticky buns. Zoey couldn't remember ever eating such a wonderful breakfast, at least not in a long time.

They spent the rest of the day walking around Discovery Park and enjoying steaming bowls of clam chowder. Damien even bought her and Camille a pair of sterling silver earrings from a street vendor. Finally, after a long day in the city, the three of them took the bus back to their place.

Damien froze when he flipped on the lights. An older man stood before them holding a gun. His other hand leaned on a wooden cane.

"Dad, what're you doing here?" Damien asked. "How'd you find us?"

"Hi Damien," the man said. "The question is, what are you doing here—and why haven't you given me those girls?"

Damien started to lunge at him, but two other men appeared and blocked him. Lead pipes in their hands. The last thing Zoey saw was the men clubbing his body on the ground.

CHAPTER 10

Aidan wanted to believe that what Leah had told him was true.

If a school administrator was changing students' records for sex, he had one of the best local stories of all time. But on the other hand, Aidan's skeptical instincts kicked in. Maybe Leah had made the whole thing up. Only one way to find out—public records.

Leah had given him thirteen names of girls from South County High School. If he and Cal could confirm that these teenagers were being withdrawn and then re-enrolled from the school's database, it could at least help prove a data-rigging scandal. Proving a sex crime would take more work, but there had to be a way.

At that moment, Aidan felt guilty. He had just received evidence of a crime, and he thought first about his story. As a journalist, Aidan knew he had to protect his sources, but he also had an obligation to tell the police.

So he called Briggs. "I may have something for you."

"You've got something for me?" the deputy asked with a chuckle. "That's a first. Usually it's the other way around."

Aidan laughed. "I know, but I just talked to that girl, Leah. Did she say much to you?"

"No," the deputy replied. "She kept her mouth shut most of the time in the interrogation room. Why are you asking anyway? What do you have?"

Aidan glanced down at the sheet of paper Leah had given him. "I've got a list of names. Leah said some administrator blackmailed her and several other girls into having sex in exchange for changing their school records. I know it sounds crazy, but I've got to look into this more."

Briggs didn't answer. Instead, Aidan just heard a deep sigh on the end of the line.

"You still there?" Aidan asked.

"Yeah, sorry," Briggs replied. "I'm just processing it all. If that's true, our investigation got ten times bigger. God, I wish we had more resources right now. We're stretched so thin."

"Well, can't you get more deputies?"

"It doesn't work that way, Ade. The sheriff has already laid off so many people. And since La Pine just became an actual city, they can't afford to hire any more for patrol. You've got my word, though. I'll keep investigating this. Can you give me that list today?"

After taking a photo of the names, Aidan brought Leah's paper to Briggs. Then he drove back to the newsroom, touched base with Mitch and decided to take a much-deserved smoke break with Cal.

The two stepped outside to the patio and lit their tobacco as the sun set. While watching his smoke rise into the air, Aidan saw a flock of geese migrating south, going some place warm. Part of him wished he could join them.

"You ready for this?" Cal asked.

"What do you mean?"

"This story," Cal continued. "Are you ready for it? Because if what that girl says is true, Mitch is going to have us work on this nonstop—in addition to all of those stupid local events. Just promise me you won't forget you have a family. No story's worth that."

"Still looking out for me," Aidan said with a smile. "But yeah, I'm ready for this."

"How do you know?"

Aidan dropped his cigarette on the concrete, crushed the butt beneath his boot and patted Cal on the back.

"Cause I'm not working any more today," he said. "In fact, I'm going home right now to take my wife dancing like I promised."

"Oh good God," Cal said. "On second thought, maybe you should work more on your story. At least you won't embarrass your wife in public."

Aidan headed home. In the back of his mind, he knew Cal was right. No story was worth that. But this was a story that had to be told.

And nothing was going to stop him until he took the last shot.

THE
SHUTTER

CHAPTER 1

The room was dark when Zoey regained consciousness. Dark and cold.

She jumped out of bed, but the feel of metal snapped her wrists back onto the mattress. Zoey shook her arms. This time she heard the sound of chains clanking. Zoey couldn't see anything, but she heard Camille whimpering in a corner of the room.

"Are you OK?" Zoey asked. "Did they hurt you?"

Her sister kept crying. Zoey got choked up as well, but she had to stay strong for Camille. Her eyes began to adjust to the room. Smelled of mildew. She figured they were in a basement because of the concrete floor and an old water heater in the corner. Zoey could also see Camille now. She lay strapped down to a bed across from her.

"Did Damien do this?" Camille asked. "Did he trap us?"

Zoey had almost forgotten about him after she passed out. But everything started coming back. She remembered seeing an older man who asked about them.

Just then, someone banged hard on the basement door. She froze. The banging continued. Zoey heard a door creak open and saw feet stepping down the stairs into the room. A faint sliver of light crept in, but then vanished as the door shut. In the darkness Zoey could make out the figure of a man.

He came slowly down the steps with a wooden cane, one clank at a time. There was an air about him. Maybe it was his black leather jacket or slick white hair, but he looked suave—and yet savage at the same time.

"Hello girls," he said with a voice smooth as molasses. "I'm sorry we had to meet like this. I was hoping to welcome you before in person—especially after sending all those texts."

Zoey yanked so hard on her chains it felt like the metal would break her bones. But she didn't care.

She couldn't stand the thought of meeting *him*.

"My name's Gabriel," the man continued. "I'm Damien's dad."

Gabriel waited for a response, but Zoey just stared at him. "What, he never mentioned me much?"

Zoey shook her head.

"I'm not surprised," Gabriel said. "He's always been a pussy. But the fact is, Damien works with me. We have a business, and we want you to be part of it."

Gabriel walked to another corner of the room and turned on a small light. Then the man came back to Zoey. She could hear his cane getting closer and closer.

Clank. Clank.

She hated that sound. Bumps spread across her skin.

"See that light over there?" Gabriel asked. "Do you know what that is?"

Neither spoke.

"It's a video camera," Gabriel continued. "I know you girls haven't been told this much before, but you're beautiful. You could both be models some day, and I want to help you with that."

Zoey laughed at him. "By taking more naked photos of us?"

A spark illuminated the man's clean-shaven face as he lit a cigar. The harsh smell mixed with the mold and must of the room and made her feel nauseous.

"That's what I love about you," Gabriel said. "You get right to the point. But no, we're not going to take any more photos. Those have already done really well. We want you to help us with a video project."

This time, Camille spoke. "You mean a porno?"

"No, pornos are for poor, low-class scum who just want to get off," Gabriel said. "I create art. And that's where I need your help."

Zoey looked at Camille.

"Will you give us those photos back?" Zoey asked. "And promise not to show them to anyone at school?"

Gabriel took a long drag on his cigar.

"That all depends on how hard you're willing to work," he said. "You're going to have to earn those back, especially since you tried running away. But if you get good—and I know you will—we can move on to some better projects. You have the potential to earn so much money. It'll be a whole new life for you."

Gabriel paused, took another puff and waited for them to answer.

"Are you some kind of pimp?" Zoey asked.

"That's one way to put it," Gabriel said with a wink. "But I prefer to think of myself more as a businessman. No, a philanthropist. After all, I own a gentleman's club that gives so much back to the community. I help single moms earn a living, you know."

Zoey rolled her eyes. Part of her didn't want to find out the answer, but she knew she had to ask.

"How long has Damien been working for you? Did he become my friend just so he could bring us to you?"

Gabriel shook his head.

"He didn't bring you to me," the pimp said. "That's why we had to intervene. He had no clue we were following you. Sometimes Damien gets soft, but he's still a hustler—just like me. That'll never change, because I've taught him well. Now, what do you think of my offer?"

Both girls looked at each other. Then they flipped him off at the same time.

"I really wish you hadn't done that," the pimp said. "As I told you, I'm a patient and caring man—but I hate it when my girls say no."

Step by step, Gabriel climbed the stairs with his cane. Zoey wanted to snatch that piece of wood from his hand and beat him with it. But whatever hope she had died when she heard him bolt the door.

Zoey pulled again on her chains, but nothing happened. She looked around. No windows. The only opening came from a small white drainpipe that swallowed shallow water from the floor.

For the next minute, Zoey thought as Camille moaned in the corner. She knew they wouldn't have time to get out of the chains. But she also knew they had one advantage. Zoey couldn't believe she hadn't thought of it before. She whispered to Camille what to do and shut her eyes.

Gabriel came down the steps again. Zoey wanted to look, but she knew lying still was her only hope. She could hear the pimp walking toward her. Now she could smell him. Feel his hands on her hair. Say her name. Zoey snapped. Her teeth chomped on Gabriel's fingers, and the taste of blood filled her mouth.

"Fuck," he screamed. "You little bitch."

For a while the pimp just stared at Zoey, circling her bed like a shark. Then he wrapped his hand with a handkerchief and walked over to Camille with a plastic red jug.

"Let's try talking to your sister," Gabriel said. "Some of the johns—actually, a lot of our clients—have been looking for something new. They're getting tired of the same old cunts, so we figured a retard would do the trick."

Camille's whimpering grew louder. Zoey lunged against her chains so hard she felt the bedpost shake.

"Get away from my sister," Zoey screamed with renewed strength. "I'll kill you if you touch her."

The pimp circled back to her bed. Zoey just sat there. Head spinning. Heart pounding. As Gabriel got closer, she regained her senses and tried punching him with her handcuffed hands. Zoey hit one of his cheeks. The next moment, she felt a ringing in her ears as the pimp's cane struck her in the head. Zoey closed her eyes and waited for him to kill her. She hoped it would be quick.

But instead of touching her, Gabriel walked over to Camille's bed and lit a match. Zoey remained still. The pimp lit another match and blew it out. Then he picked up the plastic red jug. Unscrewed the lid. And poured some liquid on the ground beneath Camille's feet.

"Stop it," Zoey said, smelling gasoline.

This time, Gabriel lit two matches and dropped both of them on the ground. Within seconds, she could see smoke rising near Camille's mattress. Zoey writhed as hard as she could against her chains, but they remained fastened to the bedposts. The pimp sat next to her.

"I've always wondered what it's like to watch a little girl burn," he said. "Never thought I'd be so turned on."

"Please, don't do this," Zoey said.

The fire continued to spread. It licked Camille's feet. She could smell burning hair and hear her sister screaming.

"I'll do it," Zoey said. "I'll do it."

The pimp grabbed a fire extinguisher by the bed and sprayed it around Camille.

"Good," he said. "I knew you would. Now get some rest. It's going to be a long night."

As soon as Gabriel left, Zoey called out to Camille. No answer. Zoey called again. This time, she heard a faint moan. The door opened.

"Zoey," someone said from above the stairs. "It's me."

She watched Damien limp down the steps, cringing with each movement. He made his way over to Camille first and looked at her feet.

"Thank God," Damien said. "The fire barely touched her."

"What'd you do to us?" Zoey asked.

"I didn't do anything," Damien replied. "I had no clue he was following us. I swear to God."

Zoey scowled at him. "Is Gabriel really your dad?"

Damien took a deep breath and nodded.

"I never meant for you to get hurt," he said. "I've been trying to run away from his fucking gang for years."

As Zoey's eyes continued to adjust to the darkness, she could see that Damien had a black eye and a bump on his head. There were tears beneath his eyes, too. Maybe he was telling the truth.

"You were supposed to be my last girl," Damien said. "But after I met you and your mom and your sister, I just couldn't take it anymore."

"Did you recruit Leah, too?"

Damien rubbed his bruised head.

"No, some asshole at school did that," he said. "Most of the girls we get come from really fucked up families. But we needed a bottom girl. A recruiter. Someone with a little more money who could throw parties to scope out our next girl and blackmail her with photos. Leah's been working for us since freshman year. We found her like we find all of the girls—runaways, mostly."

"How many are there?" Zoey asked.

Damien didn't speak.

"I said, how many?"

"More than a dozen. I started to lose track a long time ago."

"Oh my God. That's fucking sick. How could you do that?"

"I don't want to," Damien said. "My dad forced me into it, OK? I've tried leaving so many times, but each time he..."

Damien bit his lip.

"He what?" Zoey asked.

Damien lifted up his shirt to reveal a long scar that spanned most of his back.

"Dad's gang did it with a hunting knife," Damien said. "Five of them pinned me to the ground and carved it into my back."

For a long time, Zoey remained silent. Then she decided to tell him about her own dad. And what he did. That Night.

"I was twelve," Zoey said. "That's when Dad raped me."

Zoey looked at Damien, her eyes locked on his to see if he would flinch or glance the other way. But he didn't. He just kept listening. And for the first time, Zoey felt like someone could relate to her hell.

"Dad came home drunk again from cooking crystal," she continued. "But this time, he seemed different. This time, he looked extra drunk. Maybe high. I don't know. All I know is that when he came through my bedroom door, something was wrong.

"It wasn't the beating. Dad had hit me so many times before. But this time, he told me to take my clothes off. And so I did. I knew I should've screamed. Should've yelled. But it was Dad, you know? My own fucking father. So I froze.

"At one point, it really hurt. I tried to get away. But that's when he pulled the knife. Told me that if I did anything, he'd slice my throat.

"Twice I almost passed out because of the pain. Once it hurt so bad I just couldn't take it anymore, so I shoved my fist into his mouth. Broke a tooth. I don't think he meant to cut me, but the tip stabbed right beneath my left eye. Thought I was blind. There was so much blood.

"Thank God, Mom woke up. She never saw Dad on top of me, but I think she knew something was wrong. And she's been trying to get us away from him ever since."

Damien looked straight into Zoey's eyes. She wiped them, but most of the eyeliner was gone around her scar.

Suddenly, the door opened again.

"You done yet, Damien? We don't have all day."

Zoey recognized Gabriel's voice. And she hated it.

"I said, are you done yet?"

Damien looked at the camera in the corner. Then he looked at Zoey and Camille. Finally, he faced his dad walking down the stairs.

"I'm not going to do it."

"What the fuck are you talking about?" the pimp asked.

"I told you, I'm done."

Gabriel walked up to Damien and stared down his son. "This isn't an option, boy. You made your choice a long time ago. Now go fuck them before we fuck you."

Two other men came down the steps and surrounded Damien with lead pipes. For a second, nobody moved. The room felt blacker, suffocating her like a blanket. He just kept his eyes locked on hers.

Then Damien turned around and glared at his dad. "No."

The first strike hit him hard in the head. He didn't even have a chance to defend himself. The second and third hits crushed his legs. And the fourth and fifth blows struck his back.

"Stop it," Zoey screamed. "You're killing him."

The men carried Damien's body up the stairs as Gabriel walked over to the camera and turned the light back on again. Then he grabbed a needle and sat by Zoey's bed with a bag.

"You're going to like this," Gabriel said. "It'll help season you. Make you feel real happy. In fact, once you mix sex with meth, it's impossible to stop. Eventually, you're going to want more and more—and the only place you'll be able to get it for free is from us."

Zoey squirmed when the cold needle pricked her skin. She felt the burn of the liquid spreading through her body.

"Your first client is going to come over here soon," the pimp added. "Act like you're enjoying it. Because if you don't, we're going to stop the camera, and he's going to hurt you. Understand?"

She understood. In fact, Zoey had never felt so focused in her life. Her whole body screamed with energy. She wanted to break through her chains and run around the room.

"Don't worry," Gabriel continued. "I know you're afraid, because I know about your father."

How does he know that?

"I know a lot about you, Zoey, and all of your problems at home."

Has he been to our trailer?

"In fact, we've been watching you for a while now at school, and we thought you'd like to play our little games with us. We're going to start with some porn. Then we're going to play the real game—the life."

Zoey didn't know what that meant, but she felt sick to her stomach. "Where's Damien?"

"He'll live," Gabriel replied. "Like I said, he can be such a pussy sometimes, especially around young girls. Someday he'll realize it's just business."

Zoey could still hear him, but her eyes fluttered from one object to the next. She became fixated on the white drainpipe that still licked up water from the floor.

"Now listen carefully," the pimp continued. "You're going to be playing a lot of games with my gang whether you like it or not. If you don't play along—and I swear to God if you ever rat on us—we're going to kill your whore of a mom."

Zoey knew she was about to black out. She could feel another man's cold hands taking her jeans off. Then her bra. And panties. The last thing Zoey saw was the clear white light of the camera shining on her naked body. It made her feel warm. And it gave her one last surge of strength.

"Fuck you," she said.

That was the last thing Zoey remembered before the camera started rolling.

CHAPTER 2

W hen Aidan's alarm went off the next morning, he couldn't
get out of bed.

His whole body still ached from dancing with his wife.
Normally, he exercised at least three times a week by mountain
biking, but this was different. Aidan pulled muscles he didn't
even know existed.

Then he remembered his meeting.

Mitch demanded that he and Cal attend the editors' morning briefing to discuss their next steps in the investigation. Aidan
started preparing a full meal of orange juice, egg whites and
black coffee, but quickly realized he wouldn't have enough time.
That dancing had gotten the better of him. After kissing his wife
and daughter goodbye, he grabbed a bagel and sped to the newsroom. He arrived just in time.

"This is Aidan and Cal," Mitch said as he introduced them

to a small room of editors and the publisher himself, Donald Undershaw. "I think most of you've met them before. As I mentioned yesterday, they're the ones digging into this investigation. So, what do you boys have?"

Aidan looked at Cal, who nodded for him to speak.

"Not much," Aidan said as he dusted the snow from his curly black hair. "Right now, all we've confirmed is that a school records administrator spent taxpayer money at a strip club during work hours. We also have a girl from South County High who claims that this administrator blackmailed her and more than a dozen other girls into having sex with men at the club or at a motel across the street—all in exchange for changing their records."

"What evidence do you have so far?" the publisher asked.

"A list of names," Aidan said. "From the victim."

"An *alleged* victim," Undershaw said.

"Excuse me?" Aidan asked.

"She's an alleged victim," the publisher repeated. "Remember, there's no proof that anything actually happened yet. For all we know, she could've made up the whole goddam story. I'm not putting our paper at risk of libel unless you boys get some more evidence, you hear? Plus, remember this is a family paper for Christ's sake. I don't think our readers and advertisers want to see a lot of stories about high school girls getting raped."

Aidan didn't know what to say. He could take shit from Mitch, but at least he had the balls to pursue a good story—no matter where the truth led.

"What Don meant to ask you is how you're going to pursue this story," Mitch said, winking at Aidan. "Obviously, we can't publish anything right now, so what's your plan?"

"We're going to start with the records," Cal said. "We've already put in a request to the district to get their student stats for the last few years. As you know, the records are confidential. But Ade and I can cross reference our list of names with the number of suspicious attendance records that may have been withdrawn from the system and then re-enrolled into it."

Cal looked at Aidan and then continued. "If this 'alleged' victim is telling the truth, there should be more than a dozen instances of this data rigging. We're assuming that these girls may look good on paper, but probably aren't going to school that often, so we're also going to have to try and talk to them in person."

"And what if they won't talk?" Undershaw asked. "What if they won't help you?"

"One of them will," Aidan said. "It only takes one to talk and bring this bastard down. Sorry, I should've said *alleged* bastard."

With that, Aidan and Cal left the room. As he got a cup of coffee from the break room, Cal came up to him.

"Bro, you've got to be more careful. Seriously, one of these days you're going to get fired."

Aidan scowled at him.

"Actually, I'm just bullshitting you," Cal said. "Good job in there. It's about time someone put Don in his place. He's so concerned about advertisers these days. So, you ready to get started?"

For the next hour, Aidan and Cal researched as much as they could about the girls and their families. They checked old news stories and photos. Looked up prior arrests. Even researched high school sports stats. But nothing came up. Every lead went cold.

Then Mitch walked up to their desks.

"We've got a hole in Local," he said. "A story just fell

through, so unless you boys have any more leads, I need you and Cal to cover Santa Paws for tomorrow's paper."

"Excuse me?" Aidan asked.

"Santa Paws," Mitch replied. "It's that annual fundraiser by the Humane Society. I don't know much about it, but we don't have anything else right now. Also, Ade, get me another weather photo. There's supposed to be a big snowstorm coming."

Aidan and Cal both groaned.

After grabbing a quick coffee at Strictly Organic, the two drove to Mirror Pond, where they took some shots of children chasing drakes by the frozen water. Another front-page photo. Then they headed north to the Deschutes County Fair & Expo Center for Santa Paws. Despite the cold, both men took the opportunity to roll the windows down and light their favorite tobacco.

Cal smoked his usual briar pipe, while Aidan lit another black Natural American Spirit cigarette. The two vapors smelled surprisingly good together, a blend of wood and rum. Once they arrived at the fair, the smell of damp dog hair and the sound of purring cats immediately overwhelmed them.

Aidan snapped shots of a Miniature Schnauzer-Silky Terrier mix that squirmed as its owner forced the dog onto the lap of a middle-aged man wearing some sort of Santa Claus suit. He looked more like a drunk elf.

Clearly, the man was not enjoying his job. Neither were Aidan or Cal. But they kept taking photos and interviewing random strangers who waited in line to get their pets' pictures taken with reindeer ears and Father Fucking Christmas.

"So why'd you take your cats here?" Cal asked a woman with two felines in each of her arms and two more that walked on leashes beside her.

"Oh we just love coming each year," she said. "I know my neighbors like to call me 'The Cat Lady,' but I just love my little pussies."

Aidan could tell Cal was trying hard not to laugh. "And what are your cats' names?"

"Which one?" she cackled while licking one of her cat's wet noses. "Well let's see, there's Sally the Siamese, Cory the Calico, and–"

Before the woman could finish, a Great Dane charged at her cats and almost swallowed one whole were it not for the flash that Aidan used to get the action. Apparently the light disoriented the dog. But that didn't stop the woman's cats from huddling together behind a box in the corner of the room, forming what looked like one giant ball of fur that swarmed and writhed like a hairy wave.

He snapped a few photos, but a phone call from Mitch saved him.

"Believe it or not, your records just came," he said. "You boys about done?"

Aidan and Cal sped back to the newsroom. Not surprisingly, most of the data was a complete mess. It was in an old version of Access and took them hours just to sort through all of the cells and categorize everything in a format that actually made sense.

But once they finished, Aidan and Cal discovered more than a dozen suspicious cases of what looked like withdrawn and re-enrolled students with near-perfect grades and attendance records. Now they just had to knock on some doors to confirm if those students matched the names Leah gave them.

When they tried talking to the first girl, she refused. So did the next. And the next.

In fact, every single teenager they tried interviewing either wasn't at school during the day when they should have been, or slammed the door in their faces at night when Aidan and Cal went to their homes.

Although those facts didn't prove data rigging, it did show that these were not perfect students. But they still needed someone to talk to them.

And there were only two names left on the list—Zoey and Camille.

CHAPTER 3

Zoey awoke in a panic.

The room was still dark, but this time her bed shook. As Zoey's eyes began to adjust, she saw white lights zooming past her. She yanked on the chains, only to realize her hands were free. No longer did she feel the coldness of steel cuffs cutting into her wrists.

Instead, a hand held hers. Zoey looked down and saw Camille lying asleep next to her in a van with tinted windows. She couldn't tell who was driving, but she peered outside and saw a sign. They were heading south. Back to La Pine.

Zoey's head pounded. Her mouth felt like sandpaper. And her whole body itched. When she tried shifting in her seat, she felt a stab of pain. Slowly, the memories started coming back. Zoey closed her eyes, wishing she could just disappear forever into the blackness of the night.

After she opened them, the sun had started peeking over the mountains. Apparently it was morning. But she didn't care. Whatever energy Zoey had received from the crank had started to wear off. Now she just felt depressed and exhausted. Camille stirred. She opened her eyes for a second and then lay her head back down on Zoey's shoulder.

"What's happening?" Camille whispered.

"Nothing. Go back to sleep."

Zoey caressed Camille's frizzy hair, hoping to God that was true.

"Is Camille going to die?" her sister asked.

Zoey wanted to cry so badly, but fought back the urge. Instead, she just held her sister tighter.

The girls slept for the rest of the trip. Once they reached La Pine hours later, Zoey could tell that Gabriel was driving the van. They pulled up to Baldy's Truck Stop, and the pimp got out of the vehicle. He locked the doors and waited until Damien pulled into the parking lot in his own car. He looked awful. Bruises blackened his entire face. Zoey couldn't tell what they were saying to each other. Every now and then Damien looked over at their van, but she knew he couldn't see them through the dark windows.

Finally, they quit talking and Damien gave one last glance at the van. She couldn't tell for sure, but it looked like he saw her for a moment. Then he drove away. Gabriel returned and let them out of the vehicle.

"All right girls, you're home," he said. "Well, close enough. You'll have to walk a ways from here. I hope you understand. Now, do you remember what we told you?"

Zoey shook her head. She barely remembered anything from last night.

"If you talk to anybody about us, we'll give those photos to everyone at school," the pimp said. "And don't you even think about calling the cops. They won't believe a whore and a retard. Plus, one of them works for me, so the moment he finds out, we'll kill your mom. Understand?"

They both nodded.

"Good, now I don't want to be such a drag," Gabriel continued. "So here's a little thank you for all your hard work last night."

He handed them each a necklace.

"You'll both look gorgeous in it," the pimp said. "All right, I'm going to give you your phones back now, too. Sorry I didn't trust you with them this weekend. Make sure you keep these on you at all times, OK? I'll see you soon."

Gabriel handed them their phones and then drove away. For a few minutes Zoey and Camille just stood there. Shaking. Not knowing what to do. They were both so cold. So tired. So scared.

The sisters walked home in silence. Zoey still didn't feel safe there after what had happened with their dad, but they didn't have any other choice. Their trailer was still safer than the streets.

Plus, part of Zoey just didn't give a shit about anything anymore. Something inside her had died. She felt like a phantom, a ghost or shadow trying to peer through glass into the world of the living. Zoey couldn't hear. Feel. Smell. Or taste. She saw snow falling, but didn't feel cold. She watched trucks drive by, but couldn't hear their engines.

The whole world seemed to fade before her glassy eyes into a hazy, black and white photo of some distant memory. The only sense she had was the remembrance of the last words Gabriel spoke before tossing them back onto the streets like a heap of garbage:

I'll see you soon.

Zoey had heard so many brutal words last night from Gabriel, but those four cut into her ears like cold steel. What did "soon" mean? Later today? Tomorrow? The next day? Multiple times a day?

A splash of ice water from a passing truck jolted Zoey back into what felt like a foreign country. Her body began to shake uncontrollably. She could barely walk. But Zoey and Camille kept limping along Highway 97.

By the time the girls got back to their trailer park, the late afternoon sun was shining unusually bright. She could hear the red-tailed hawks screeching and downy woodpeckers chirping among the ponderosa pines, which normally made her happy. But today they just made her long for a world she could never re-enter.

That's when Zoey saw the fire. Her mom sat on a lawn chair bundled in blankets near a pile of wood that burned hot orange and sent wisps of smoke into the sky. Beside her mom sat Josiah and his own mother, Marge.

Josiah—she had almost forgotten about him until he sprang from his seat and hugged her until she couldn't breathe.

"Where've you been?" Jo asked. "We've been so worried."

She and Camille couldn't find a single word. Zoey just clutched Josiah. She cried until black eyeliner bled onto one of his old flannel shirts. She loved that familiar warmth and feel. Ella and Marge surrounded them as well. They hugged and laughed and cried at the same time.

"Thank God you're OK," Ella told her daughters.

Zoey and Camille just sank into their mother's arms and

sobbed even harder.

"Come sit by the fire," Ella said. "Our space heater broke last night."

The five sat down on lawn chairs. Zoey tried to get comfortable, but she kept squirming in her seat. She saw that everyone was staring at her, so she tried to make conversation.

"What're you drinking, Mom?" Zoey asked, noticing that for once she didn't have a can of Natty Light in her hand.

"Tea," Ella said. "Marge bought me some. Tastes like shit, but I'm done drinking beer. Want some?"

Zoey shook her head, and everyone just stared at the embers. Nobody spoke. Too much to ask. Too much to say. So Zoey sat by the fire and inhaled wood smoke. It burned her eyes and throat. But she was too tired to move and too tired to care. Zoey knew she couldn't tell them what had happened, but she had to think of something.

"I'm sorry we ran away," Zoey said. "We just needed to get away from–"

"Stop talking, honey," her mom interrupted. "It's my fault. We can talk about it later. You girls just relax right now. All I care about is that you're safe and back home. You don't have to worry about your dad anymore. I called the cops on his ass, so he should be in jail for a long time."

Zoey swallowed hard. She wanted so badly to scream, to tell her mom and Josiah everything. How they weren't safe. How Leah had recruited them. How Gabriel had kidnapped them. How they had photographed them. Then filmed them. How Damien was the son of a pimp.

But she couldn't.

Gabriel had promised to kill their mom if she talked or

went to the cops. Zoey didn't know if she believed him, but she'd seen enough photos to know that he wasn't fucking around. So Zoey just leaned back in her lawn chair and stared at the fire.

Finally, she stood up. "I'm going to take a shower."

"That sounds good, honey," her mom said. "We'll have some food ready when you're done."

Zoey slinked back to the trailer. She locked the bathroom door, stared at herself in the mirror and then burst into tears. She looked sick. Her hair twisted in every direction, and her eyes dripped eyeliner down her cheeks like black blood.

One at a time, she removed her pieces of clothing, fearing what she would see. Blotches of deep blue and purple splattered her skin. She stepped into the shower after it heated up. Despite what had happened with her dad, this was still her sanctuary. Zoey relaxed as the hot water caressed her skin, washing away dried blood and sweat that disappeared forever down the drain. Half an hour later, she heard someone banging on the bathroom door.

"You drown in there or something?" her mom asked. "Come on, food's almost ready."

Zoey stepped out of the shower. She heard another knock on the door. "Coming."

"It's me," Josiah said. "Can we talk?"

Zoey threw on some sweatpants and a long-sleeve T-shirt. Then she opened the door for him.

"You're a hot mess," he said, wiping snot from her nose with his sleeve. "Your mom told me what happened with your dad. I've never seen her so torn up. She's really sorry for the whole thing. And I think it's real this time."

Zoey nodded.

"So, what happened?" Josiah asked. "Where'd you go?"

"Just hold me," Zoey said, clutching his thick, strawberry-blond hair.

They started walking toward the kitchen, where the sound of crackling bacon revived her a little. She could hear laughter and smell strong coffee. Marge scrambled eggs as Ella poured pancake batter upon a skillet. Her mom had never been a good cook, not even when she was sober.

"Feel better?" Ella asked as she raced toward her in such hurry and excitement that she accidently spilled the pancake batter onto the floor. "Shit."

"Yeah," Zoey lied. "What're you guys making?"

"Breakfast for dinner," Marge said. "I made the bacon just the way you like it—extra crispy."

Zoey crunched into the sweet meat, feeling the warm grease burst into her mouth and soothe her throat. She ate five more pieces before Jo and her mom snatched the plate from her.

"Calm down," her mom said.

"Oh, let the girl eat," Marge said. "She looks half starved. Just make sure you save room for dessert."

For the briefest of moments, Zoey relaxed. She had never felt so loved as she did that night. After finishing an early dinner, they played games until she fell asleep with her head on the table.

———

During the middle of the night, Zoey awoke next to Camille and her mom in bed.

She was lying curled up next to them, something she hadn't done since grade school. It used to be one of her favorite things as a little girl, long before That Night.

Zoey loved the feel of her mom's warm body as it gently rose and fell with each breath. She had almost forgotten that sensation. But now she reveled in it. Her mom stirred and woke up as well. Then she stroked the girls' hair and started to sing them softly back to sleep:

This little light of mine,
I'm gonna let it shine,
Let it shine.
Let it shine.
Let it shine.

Once Ella finished, she looked straight into her daughters' eyes as she held their hands.

"Look, girls. I know what happened."

Zoey froze. She glared at her mom, searching her eyes.

"I've been around your dad long enough to know you tried some crank," Ella said. "But, I just wanted to say that I'm here for you. I know I haven't been the best mom, but I'm trying to change. What Ricky did to you, I don't know, it's like it woke me up out of a deep sleep or something."

Her mom didn't have a clue. But Zoey had to tell her the truth. Despite the danger, Zoey knew it was the only way she and Camille could escape. She had already tried keeping the pictures from Leah's party a secret, only to be forced into a porno. So she decided to tell her mom what had happened.

Everything. From beginning to end.

After she finished, Ella's knuckles looked like pure white bone as they gripped her daughters' hands. "Oh, God. Oh, baby.

Girls, we've got to call the cops right now."

Her mom reached for the phone, but Zoey knocked it out of her hands.

"Haven't you been listening to anything I just said? He'll kill us if he finds out."

"Then I'm going to kill him. Who is he? What the hell does he look like?"

"Mom, you can't do that. He'll kill you first."

"I don't give a shit," Ella said. "I'm going to get you and Camille out of this. Now, think very carefully. What does he look like?"

Zoey thought for a while.

"I'll tell you," she finally said. "But only if you promise me you won't do something stupid. We can figure this out together, but you can't go trying to stop him. He's too dangerous."

Ella promised. As Zoey explained Gabriel's wooden cane, black jacket and white hair, her mom started shaking.

"That fucking bastard," Ella said. "I'm going to fucking kill him."

"You know him? How could you possibly know him, Mom?"

"Because he's my boss."

"At the bar?"

"No, at Jugs," Ella said. "I'm sorry, girls. I shouldn't have lied to you about where I worked, but I didn't want you to know. I couldn't get a job anywhere else."

Zoey and Camille embraced their mom.

Just then, Zoey felt her phone vibrate. "It's *him*. He wants us to meet again tonight."

"Good," her mom replied. "Because I have an idea. And I think I know someone who can help."

CHAPTER 4

That same throbbing beat greeted Aidan as he pulled back into the parking lot of Jugs.

God, he hated this place. It still smelled of stale smoke, cheap liquor and body odor. He sat at the same table by the back. Another girl walked up to him, but he motioned her away. Like last time, Aidan felt awkward and out of place. He watched some young men in business suits throw dollar bills at a woman on stage. Then Aidan caught Ella's attention. She winked at him.

"What do you need?" Ella asked in a seductive voice, starting her tease.

Aidan tried to go along with the routine, but he kept glancing nervously around him.

"Shouldn't we have met somewhere less public?" he whispered.

Ella thrust herself closer to him.

"It's the safest place," she said. "Boss is always watching us, no matter where we are. But this is the last place he'd expect us to meet. So, just act like you're enjoying it."

Aidan sat back and tried to relax as Ella leaned in even closer. She pretended to kiss his ear, but started whispering into it instead.

"I called you because of my daughters," Ella said. "Gabriel—the man who runs this club—has been using them for sex. I just found out. My girls are waiting in the car, so can you come out and talk to them now?"

"What are your daughters' names?" Aidan asked.

"Zoey and Camille."

Aidan couldn't believe what he was hearing. "Oh my God. They're on the list."

"What list?"

"Your daughters are on a list I got from a girl at school," Aidan replied. "I talked to her after the police released her. Holy shit. She told me she's been helping recruit teens at school, and the administrator has been changing their records. He must be working for Gabriel."

Ella leaned back and looked confused. "Wait, what are you talking about?"

"It doesn't matter," Aidan said. "All that matters is that your daughters are in serious trouble, but I can help them if they're willing to talk. Do you think they will be?"

It looked like Ella was holding back tears. She leaned in close again and started whispering into his other ear.

"Yeah, especially Zoey," Ella said. "That's why I called you tonight. I don't know what else to do. We can't go to the cops, cause..."

Before Aidan could answer, he saw an older man coming

toward them with a wooden cane, and a cigar dangling from his lips.

"Good evening," the man said. "I'm Gabriel, the owner of this place. You two seem pretty chatty tonight. Actually, the last couple times I've seen you here."

"I'm just here to get a lap dance," Aidan replied.

The old man inhaled some smoke and blew it onto Aidan's face.

"Who the fuck are you?" he asked. "And what exactly do you want with my girl?"

The room became silent. Aidan glanced around and noticed that some of the other men were staring at him. A few got up and left the club. His stomach twisted like a knot.

"I don't want any trouble," Aidan said.

"You've already got some," the man replied as he motioned to a bouncer. "You've scared off some of my customers and made one of my girls nervous, so I suggest you leave now before things get worse."

A bouncer lifted Aidan from behind, dragged him past the now completely silent stage and shoved him out the door. He stumbled back to his car and started calling Mitch, but Ella came right up to him again and handed him Zoey's cell number on a piece of paper.

"Promise me you'll protect them," Ella said. "No matter what happens."

Aidan grabbed the paper from Ella's hand.

"I promise," he said.

For a moment, Ella looked relieved. Then her face turned pale. "Oh God, he's coming again. I've got to get back. Can I call you tomorrow?"

Aidan nodded as he dialed Mitch again and sped out of the parking lot to tell him everything that had happened. Once he got onto the highway, he saw sheriff cars speeding past him. Heading toward La Pine. Then another call came in. It was Briggs.

"I told you I'd keep my word if anything happened," the deputy said. "Meet me at Jugs right now. Man, have I got a scoop for you."

CHAPTER 5

Zoey heard a scream.

As Ella had told them to do, she and Camille were still waiting in their mom's car at the parking lot of Baldy's Truck Stop, right across the street from Jugs. But when people started screaming and racing from the strip club, Zoey got out of the car.

"Don't go," Camille begged. "Mom said to stay here."

Zoey ignored her sister and raced toward the club, looking for her mom in the sea of strippers and men who crashed over each other as they spilled into the darkness. She tried asking a few people questions, but nobody knew what had happened. Everybody just kept coming out of the club.

Everybody except for her mom.

Zoey's heart sank as she heard sirens wail and saw bright lights speeding toward them. Several sheriff cars swerved around the wave of people and shot toward the back of the club. Zoey followed them until she ran into Damien.

"What happened?" Zoey asked.

"Zoey, please, you need to go now. You shouldn't be here."

"Damien, what happened?"

"I'm serious. You need to go—now."

Zoey saw a woman lying face down on the ground, her neck contorted. She raced toward the body, but Damien stopped her before she could reach the lifeless form. Clawing and scratching at his face, Zoey tried to escape Damien's grip, but he held her tight.

Finally, she fell into a heap on the black asphalt, pounding her fists on the ground. She couldn't think. Couldn't breathe. Saw spots.

Blacked out.

The high desert sun had just started to rise when Zoey smelled hot cocoa.

For the briefest of moments, she sighed. Everything had just been a nightmare. But then she remembered her mom's neck. Bent backwards. Zoey could feel sweat dripping down her back. Her whole body shook and itched again.

"Hi dear," Marge said as she sat down next to Zoey on a cot. "You probably don't want to talk right now, so I just brought you some food in case you got hungry."

Marge handed her a slice of toast and a white foam cup filled with cocoa. Zoey bolted up from bed.

"Is Mom...? Did she...?"

As soon as Marge nodded her head, Zoey collapsed back

onto the cot.

"The police are still trying to figure everything out," Marge said. "They've tried talking to you, but you've been in too much shock."

Zoey felt dizzy again. "Why am I at your trailer?"

"Your mom had a will," Marge said. "And she decided when you ran away that she wanted you to live here with us in case anything ever happened to her."

Tears formed beneath Marge's eyes.

"Your dad's still in jail of course," Marge continued. "So I brought all your belongings over to our trailer, except for Quill. I'm sorry, but we couldn't find her anywhere. Must've finally run off."

Zoey didn't know what to say. She just kept staring at the ground.

Marge put her arm around her. "I'll let you be alone now. Just promise me you'll eat that food. I'll be right here, so let me know if you need anything else."

"Where's Camille?" Zoey asked.

"Your sister's been crying in the bathroom all morning," Marge said. "I tried getting her to come out, but she locked the door. Maybe you should try."

After Marge left the trailer, Zoey lay down on her cot. She thought about sitting up, but that seemed exhausting. So she just remained motionless. For the next few minutes, it felt like a thick black fog was seeping into the trailer and poisoning her mind. She had never felt so depressed since That Night.

Normally she had a hard time dragging her body out of bed. But today was different. Her whole body ached, and she needed something to fix that. Yearned for something. Craved something.

Zoey remembered some of Gabriel's last words to her:

You're going to like this. It'll help season you. Make you feel real happy. In fact, once you mix sex with meth, it's impossible to stop. Eventually, you're going to want more and more—and the only place you'll be able to get it for free is from us.

Zoey didn't think she was addicted or anything yet, but a craving was starting to grow inside her.

That's when Zoey remembered the razor.

She hadn't done it in a while. Always hurt like hell. But growing up, cutting was the only thing that made her feel alive at times like this. For the briefest of moments, that sharp sting helped her forget all of her problems and put her in control of her own body. For years, she had been able to hide the marks from her mom by always wearing that hoodie, although Camille had walked in on her once.

Zoey sat up. She found a trash bag filled with her toiletries beneath the cot and grabbed a razor buried at the bottom. She put an extra one in her backpack. Just in case. Zoey looked around. Nobody here. Then she touched the cold steel blades to her left wrist. Her hands shook. Zoey trembled when she remembered what it felt like to slice open her skin and see blood squirting out and feel like she could die and live all over again.

All of a sudden, Zoey heard Camille screaming in the bathroom. Zoey hid her razor, raced to the bathroom and pounded on the door.

"Camille, what's going on?"

Her sister continued screaming.

Zoey pounded harder. "Dammit, Camille. Open the door."

At that moment, Josiah raced into the trailer. "What's happening?"

"I don't know," Zoey said. "Help me with the door."

Josiah slammed into it, but fell backwards. He threw his body at it again. This time, he heard something break. Josiah tried a third time and crashed into the bathroom. There they found Camille with a razor in her own hand, writhing in pain from her wrists that oozed blood onto the mirror. Sink. And floor.

"No," Zoey said. "No, no, no."

Josiah ripped his shirt off and applied pressure to Camille's wrists. The bleeding started to slow, but soaked his shirt. Josiah didn't say anything. He just stared at her with his ash grey eyes. Zoey couldn't stand the thought of Josiah seeing her and Camille like this, so she kept her own eyes fixed on Camille's.

Finally, the blood stopped. Josiah found some gauze from an old first aid kit and wrapped her sister's wrists tight. Then he dusted snow from his orange hunting cap, revealing his curly red hair. The three of them sat down on the only couch in the trailer.

"I'm so sorry," Josiah said. "What do you want me to do?"

"Just sit here with us," Zoey said.

Josiah looked at both girls.

"We're going to find him," he said. "I hope you know that. Whoever killed your mom, we're going to track him down. And I'm going to help you."

There was a fire in Jo's eyes—one that made him look stronger and more like Damien. He sat with them for a few more minutes. As soon as Josiah left, Zoey held Camille's face and looked straight into her eyes.

"Don't you ever do that again, you hear?" Zoey said. "We just lost Mom, and I can't lose you, too. Promise me you'll never cut again. We've got to be strong together, but I can't protect you from yourself."

Camille agreed. Just then, Zoey felt her phone vibrate. There were four missed calls from Damien. She called him back.

"I'm so sorry," Damien said.

"Stop saying that," Zoey replied. "I'm so sick of people saying that. You're not sorry. Nobody's sorry, because nobody knows what the fuck this feels like."

Damien sighed into the phone. "You're right, Zoey. I don't know what this feels like. And I also don't know who killed your mom, but we're going to find out who he is and then nail that son of a bitch."

Zoey didn't respond.

"Now, I know this isn't good timing," Damien said. "But Dad needs you and your sister to turn another trick this afternoon. He also wants to talk with you and Camille about your mom. Can I pick you up somewhere?"

"How dare you," Zoey replied. "Our mom just died, and your dad wants us to keep fucking? We can't do this anymore."

Zoey went to slam her phone against the wall, but then Damien's voice became so quiet she could barely hear him.

"Listen to me," he whispered. "I just said that because my dad came into the room. Look, I came up with an idea last night, something that may help us escape and find your mom's killer. When can we meet?"

She hung up on him.

CHAPTER 6

The high desert sun had already risen when Aidan finally got home from interviewing people at the strip club.

It was still early in the morning, but he couldn't tell the time on his watch because his hands were shaking from cold and a state of shock. The icy Cascade winds were also starting to pick up again, but that didn't stop him from trying to light a frozen cigarette.

Aidan's fingers shook even harder as they flicked the lighter. The wind kept killing his flame. Finally, he tossed the cigarette in disgust. Aidan wobbled up to their front door. He tried finding the correct key, but each time he looked down he saw Ella's face.

"Shit," Aidan said as he dropped his keys to the ground. He gave up and started knocking on the door. Nobody answered. A few more knocks and he saw Reina peeking through the glass door. "Rein, it's me."

She opened the door. "Oh my God. Ade, are you OK? What happened? I tried calling you a dozen times."

Aidan told Reina everything as she stripped off his jacket and laid him down on their couch. She wiped his face down with a cold towel.

"Did you see the murder?" she asked.

"No, thank God. But I had just talked to this woman before someone killed her. Christ, I can still see her eyes."

Aidan started shaking again.

"Why'd they kill her?" Reina asked.

"I don't know for sure, but I think it's because Cal and I are on to something with this story. The owner had one of his bouncers throw me out of the club for asking questions."

Reina started crying. "Do you hear yourself, Ade? This is getting too dangerous. You could've gotten hurt."

"That won't happen," Aidan said as he hugged his wife. "You hear me?"

Reina nodded. "Let's go to bed."

As they walked upstairs, Aidan thought about telling Reina what Ella had said about her daughters, but then his own daughter peeked her head around the bedroom door.

"Daddy, are you OK?" Indie asked.

"Yes, baby girl. Go back to sleep. Everything's fine."

As Aidan tucked Indie back into bed, he realized that what had happened to Zoey and Camille could happen to Indie or anybody else's daughter. He had to fulfill his promise to protect them. But deep down, Aidan didn't know if he could do that and also keep his promise to stay safe for his own family. Some day, Aidan knew he would have to choose.

He just didn't know when.

Aidan couldn't sleep.

He had only held Reina in bed for a few minutes before getting up to take a long, hot shower. He tried to trim his beard, but his body shook. Ella's face still haunted his mind.

"Honey, are you OK?" Reina asked as she opened the glass shower door. "Go back to bed. Call in sick or something."

"I can't, babe. Mitch will want Cal and me to brief him as soon as we get in today."

Reina dropped her nightgown and slipped into the shower with him.

"That can wait," she said, shoving him onto the seat and straddling his legs. Reina slid up and down his wet body. God, it felt so good. She kept moving faster and faster until he heard a knock on the door.

"Mommy, I'm hungry," Indie said.

"Oh, shit," Aidan muttered as Reina sprang off him and grabbed a towel.

"I'll be out in a minute, honey," she said. "Mommy's still getting ready."

"That always happens," Aidan said with a laugh. "I swear to God, it's like she knows we're having sex or something. Maybe you need to be quieter."

"I can't help myself."

That turned him on even harder.

"Come home from work early today," Reina said. "You deserve some time off."

Aidan agreed. In fact, once he got ready and started driving to work he had never wanted to head back home so soon.

He waved to the receptionist, raced up the stairs and strode through the halls of the newsroom. Nothing could take his mind off Reina—nothing except for a cryptic text message from Briggs:

Meet @ Deschutes now.

Aidan quickly touched base with Cal and Mitch about what had happened last night. He also told his editor about Briggs' text and what Ella had said about the strip club owner using her daughters for sex.

"Oh my God," Mitch said. "What do you think Briggs has for you?"

"I don't know," Aidan replied. "But I'd better go now."

Aidan started walking away, but then turned back around and looked at his editor.

"One more thing, Mitch," he said. "After I meet with Briggs, can I take the rest of the day off? I've worked so much overtime, and I really need to spend some time with my family."

Mitch's mustache seemed to bristle at the request.

"Fine, but you'd better be here first thing tomorrow morning or I'm going to have you cover the Rubber Duck Race next."

Aidan ran out to his Subaru and rolled the windows down. A cool gust of mountain air filled his nostrils with the strong smell of pine. He couldn't remember the last time he had seen the sun so bright.

When Aidan got to Deschutes Brewery, he saw Briggs already hunkered down in the back at their usual spot. It felt weird coming into their pub during the daylight. Of course, a fire was still burning in the back of the room. But there was a different bartender. And all the lights were on, illuminating some burger grease and beer spills that stained the floor.

Aidan shook Briggs' hand.

"Let's get down to business," the deputy said. "This is completely off the record, right?"

Aidan nodded. "What do you have?"

"Not much," Briggs said. "Looks like somebody snapped the stripper's neck as she was walking back to her next shift, but we don't have any suspects yet. The security camera shows the killing, but this fucker was smart. Wore gloves and a mask. Left almost no evidence at the scene."

A bartender with sloppy tattoos covering every inch of his body interrupted the men and asked if they wanted anything to drink. They both ordered coffees.

"The last time we all met here, I told you something big was going down," Briggs said. "I couldn't say much about it then. In fact, I could probably lose my job for even talking with you, but I promised you'd be the first to know."

Aidan stared at Briggs, searching his eyes. "You're not messing with me?"

"Not this time," the deputy replied. "But before I continue, tell me what you know. Last night you said you were interviewing the same stripper for a story. What was that all about?"

The bartender brought them mugs of steaming black coffee. Aidan knew it would taste good just by the rich, earthy smell of it.

Once the bartender left, Aidan leaned in close.

"We don't have much right now," he said, wrapping his hands around the warm ceramic. "All I know for sure is that the school records administrator was at the strip club in La Pine when he should've been working, and that a student from La Pine believes this administrator blackmailed her and other girls into hooking up with some guys."

Aidan took a sip of coffee and then continued.

"Two of those girls are Ella's daughters—Zoey and Camille James. As soon as I learned that, someone murdered their mom. Now I don't know about you, but that doesn't seem like a fucking coincidence."

Briggs shook his head.

"What?" Aidan asked.

"I just can't believe it," the deputy replied. "But it confirms what we've feared all along—that there actually is a sex trafficking ring right here in Bend. I still can't believe I'm saying that, but it's true."

Aidan cringed. "What do you mean by sex trafficking? I thought that kind of shit only happened in India or Thailand."

Briggs rolled his eyes.

"That's just what you people in the press like to report," the deputy said. "Sells more papers I guess. Nobody wants to read about pretty little white girls from America becoming sex slaves. But it's big business here in the states, even rural areas. Some pimps make up to two hundred grand a year per girl, depending on their quotas. Anywhere there's a demand for sex, there's always guys just waiting with a supply."

Briggs took a deep breath and then continued.

"In La Pine, Gabriel Lester is one of those suppliers, or so we think. Of course, Gabriel claims he's only a strip club owner. That's his alibi. It's a clever one, too, because we've yet to catch him in the act. But we're convinced he's laundering money through the club, which serves as his front for trafficking."

Aidan remembered that old man blowing cigar smoke on his face. Gabriel didn't strike him as a typical pimp. But then again, the only pimps Aidan could think of were from movies.

"Gabriel's what we'd call a Romeo Pimp," Briggs said. "He's violent, but he relies more on psychological manipulation to control his girls. And Gabriel isn't the only one involved. We're convinced that this records administrator—and maybe even some other guys—are recruiting girls for him."

Aidan thought for a moment. "Do you think Gabriel killed Zoey's mom?"

"No, he's too smart for that," Briggs replied. "We think he hired a hit man or something."

"So, who do you think this killer is? Why haven't you arrested anybody yet?"

Briggs slammed his mug on the table.

"This isn't fucking CSI, Ade. You can't just arrest people. You need proof, solid evidence. That takes months—sometimes even years—to gather. And at this point, we just don't have enough. In fact, we don't even have people who are talking."

Aidan apologized.

"Don't worry about it," Briggs said. "Look, our work is all about building rapport with people on the streets. But every single person we've tried interviewing—like that Leah girl—is scared shitless her pimp will kill her once the cops leave."

Suddenly, Dispatch radioed Briggs.

"You see what I mean about being stretched too thin?" Briggs asked as he took one last sip of his coffee. "I hate dog calls."

"Sounds like your version of the Pet Parade," Aidan said. "Go save that person from his neighbor's dog, Briggs."

After saying goodbye, Aidan walked back to his Subaru

and thought for a few minutes. He knew what had to be done. It wasn't exactly ethical by journalism standards, but at this point he didn't give a shit.

It was time someone paid for this crime.

CHAPTER 7

A few days after her mom's funeral, Zoey went back to school. She didn't have a clue where to start. The only homework Zoey had even tried to tackle was reading a few chapters from *Uncle Tom's Cabin*, assigned by Mr. Brookstone. But she had barely made it through the book's introduction before breaking down again.

During her first class, Zoey kept seeing her mom's casket being lowered into the ground—and Gabriel tossing a white rose into the grave. Zoey still couldn't believe that bastard had the balls to show up. He didn't say a word. Just tossed the flower. Then left. But not before smiling at her and Camille.

Making matters worse, Zoey wanted more meth. She hated herself for that fact, but Zoey had never felt so good after that needle had pricked her skin. She wanted to feel that sense of energy and euphoria again.

Finally, the bell rang.

Zoey grabbed her backpack, left her first class and bumped right into Leah. That recruiting bitch. If their school cop wasn't roaming the halls, Zoey would have punched her right in the face.

"I didn't know," Leah said. "Your mom wasn't supposed to–"

"How dare you," Zoey interrupted. "Get the fuck away from me."

Leah followed her to the locker. "I'm serious. I didn't mean for anything to happen."

"How long have you been planning this?" Zoey asked. "How many other girls have you recruited?"

"Please listen to me. I'm begging you."

"Go beg to your pimp," Zoey said. "And don't you ever talk to me or my sister again."

Zoey slammed her locker and went to Mr. Brookstone's lit class. She arrived right before her teacher started talking.

"All right, class, who can tell me the overall theme of *Uncle Tom's Cabin*?" her teacher asked.

Mr. Brookstone looked at Zoey, but she glanced the other way. She just didn't have the strength to speak.

"Well, let's hope you all actually read the chapters I assigned, because they're some of the most important in American literature. So, let me try another question. Why did Harriet Beecher Stowe write this story?"

Nobody spoke, but Zoey at least knew the answer to that question. She turned to the introduction and re-read a paragraph she had underlined:

The scenes of this story, as its title indicates, lie among a race hitherto ignored by the associations of polite and refined society ... The object of these sketches is to awaken sympathy and feeling for the African race, as they exist among us, to show their wrongs and sorrows, under a system so necessarily cruel and unjust as to defeat and do away the good effects of all that can be attempted for them, by their best friends, under it.

Mr. Brookstone put his own book down for a moment.

"Let's try something else. Who can tell me what slavery was like back then for people like Uncle Tom?"

Still nobody talked. This time, Zoey decided to raise her hand.

"A lot of masters beat their slaves," she said. "And threatened to kill their families if they tried to run away."

Her teacher smiled. "You're right, Zoey. Now, let's turn to page..."

Zoey started to tune out the world around her again. She found herself flipping aimlessly through the book until she landed on a sentence from Uncle Tom that grabbed her attention:

My life is bitter as wormwood; the very life is burning out of me. I'm a poor, miserable, forlorn drudge ... What's the use of our trying to do anything, trying to know anything, trying to be anything? What's the use of living? I wish I was dead.

Zoey kept her eyes fixed on those words:

What's the use of living? I wish I was dead.

"I'm not going to tell you how the book ends," Mr. Brookstone said, jarring Zoey back to reality. "I still want you to find that out for yourselves. But I did want to read you a quote from the author that explains how they survived until the very end:

"Another and better day is dawning ... It is a comfort to hope, as so many of the world's sorrows and wrongs have, from age to age, been lived down, so a time shall come when sketches similar to these shall be valuable only as memorials of what has long ceased to be."

The bell rang. Zoey headed for the door, but Mr. Brookstone stopped her.

"Hey, how are you holding up?" he asked.

Zoey didn't know what to say. Mr. Brookstone put his hand on her shoulder.

"I can't begin to imagine what it's like to lose a mom," her teacher said. "But let me know if there's anything I can do to help, OK?"

Zoey nodded.

"One more thing, Zoey. Keep reading. I know you like to, and there's just something about books that can help you get outside yourself and keep hope alive."

"Thanks, Mr. Brookstone. I'd better go now. I'm supposed to meet with someone to talk about my grades."

When she stepped inside the office room, a man shut the door and closed the blinds. Zoey thought that was odd. But what disturbed her even more was how he just stared at her, biting his long yellow nails and fidgeting with his hair.

"So you're Zoey," he said, not bothering to shake her hand. "I'm Walter Mortenson, the district's records administrator. I've heard so much about you...and your mom. I'm really sorry for your loss, but I have a solution that may help. That's why I came down from Bend to talk to you today."

Zoey paid attention. "I'm so far behind I don't even know where to start."

Walter wrapped what was left of his hair around one finger. "Of course, Zoey. I can help you, but I'm going to need something from you in return. I'm going to need you to stop trying to escape."

At first Zoey didn't think she had heard Walter correctly. But when he winked at her, she could feel the hair rising on her skin.

"You need to stop running away from your pimp," Walter said. "He's your Daddy now, and the only way you can keep other people from getting hurt—like your sister—is by doing what he says."

Zoey felt dizzy. She sank into a chair.

"I can fix your grades," Walter continued, "and your absences. But you need to keep your end of the bargain. And that goes for Camille, too. You see, her boss at the workshop works for the pimp, and if she ever tries escaping with you... Well, Jacob will let me know. And I don't think you want her getting hurt next time, do you? Or what about Josiah?"

Zoey shook her head and got up to leave. Walter handed her *Uncle Tom's Cabin* that she had almost left in the room.

"You can stop reading this trash," he said. "It won't matter anymore."

Zoey grabbed the book from his spindly hands and walked

out of his office. She just stood there. Holding her book.

Too shocked to move.

CHAPTER 8

A few days after Ella's funeral, Aidan went back to the school district headquarters.

He had thought about attending the funeral, but decided that he should respect the family's privacy for now. And besides, Aidan felt like what he was about to do would help avenge Ella's death. Someone had to pay. And his name was Walter Fucking Mortenson.

"Morning," Aidan said to the receptionist. "I'm Aidan Taylor with The Times. I'm here to interview the records administrator and get some photos about how great your school looked on the state's new report card."

"Well, it's about time you guys write some good news about us," the receptionist replied. "I'll see if he's available."

As the woman called him, Aidan saw people running through the halls from one place to the next. On the surface, everything looked normal.

"Mr. Taylor, you can go right on back to Walter's office. He's thrilled to meet with you."

Aidan thanked the woman, walked through the halls and knocked on his door.

"Come in."

He entered and shook the administrator's hand. It felt slimy from lotion, like the soft underbelly of a fish.

"Good to see you," Walter said. "Molly says you wanted to talk about our report card. I'm so glad you're finally doing a positive story. Sometimes, it feels like all you journalists do is record the bad stuff."

"Well, sometimes it feels like that's all that's going on."

The administrator pretended to smile. His teeth looked white as ceramic, but a piece of wet spinach was lodged between two of them. Aidan didn't bother telling him.

"So, what can I help you with?" Walter asked.

"Well, you can start by telling me why your kids' grades are so successful."

Walter sat back in his chair, put a shiny leather shoe up on his desk and cracked his knuckles.

"Where do I start? Honestly, Ade—can I call you that?—we're so successful because of the students. They're the ones who have worked so hard, not me."

"Really?" Aidan asked. "And just how hard do they actually work?"

"Oh, very hard. We have some of the best students in the district."

"Are these the same students who are having sex for grades?"

The administrator's foot slid off his desk.

"What'd you say?"

"Oh, I think you heard me."

Walter stood up and glared at him. "I don't know what you're talking about."

"Well, how about I refresh your memory?" Aidan asked. "Do these names ring a bell?"

Aidan chucked a copy of the list Leah had given him across the table. Walter glanced at the names and tossed the paper back. Then he laughed.

"It sounds like you're really desperate for news these days," the administrator said. "Or maybe you're actually starting to go crazy. I think it's best you leave now, Ade."

Aidan didn't budge.

"No, this interview isn't over yet, because there's more," he said. "I already know about your trip to see Gabriel Lester at the strip club, and one of these girls told me about your little game, plus how many more are involved. We've also cross referenced all of their names with your own records, and something doesn't quite add up. If these really are perfect students, why are they never actually at school? What are they doing during the day—or at night?"

Walter became angry. "That's none of your goddam business. And it doesn't prove anything. If these girls want to fuck for a grade, that's their choice, not mine. And you can't do anything about it."

Aidan smiled. Sometimes he couldn't believe how easy it was to catch local officials with their own words. Like shooting fish in a barrel.

Aidan pulled a tape recorder from his pocket. "I couldn't do anything about it until now."

The administrator lunged at him.

"Now you're going to beat up a photographer?" Aidan asked. "That'll make a good story in tomorrow's paper. The way I look at it, Walt—can I call you that?—you have two options. You can either say nothing to me, which means we run a front-page story exposing your corruption. Or you can tell me who you're working for and I stay quiet."

Walter paced back and forth in the room.

"Why would you stay quiet?"

As a journalist, Aidan knew he had a duty to report what he had just learned. But Aidan also knew that if he exposed the administrator now, he would never find out how many other people were involved. It would scare the big fish away.

"Because a woman was just murdered," Aidan finally said. "And I need to get to the bottom of this before someone else gets hurt."

This time, Walter sank back onto his chair. "I'll only talk if you turn that damn thing off and promise never to use my name."

Aidan pulled out the batteries and waited.

The administrator sighed and then continued. "I work for Gabriel. He's been paying me to help supply girls from school to clients by changing their records."

"How've you been changing them?"

"It's called 'scrubbing,'" Walter said. "Basically, I've been removing the records of students with low test scores and lots of absences by withdrawing them from our database and then re-enrolling them into the system. That makes us look better on the state report cards—and removes any suspicion from people on the outside."

Aidan lifted an eyebrow. "So, did you scrub the records of those thirteen girls on that list I just gave you?"

He nodded.

"And who are the clients?"

"There are so many. Teachers. Pastors. Truck drivers."

"Who else is involved?"

The administrator shook his head. Aidan scowled at him.

"Seriously, I don't know," Walter said. "Nobody knows. Look, I just deliver the girls. All I care about is the money. You think I make much here at school? Some months I can barely pay my rent."

With that, Aidan stood up and pulled the second tape recorder from his pocket that he always kept in his bag, just in case. A red recording light was flashing.

Walter's face turned as white as his teeth.

"Who else is involved?" Aidan asked again.

"Jesus, OK, I'm not the pimp's only supplier," Walter said. "A social worker is also involved. I think his name's Jacob Combs. He's been using that new sheltered workshop as a front to find autistic girls they can force into prostitution for clients who have a fetish for the disabled."

"That's better," Aidan said as he turned his second recorder off. "Now look, I'll keep my promise to stay quiet if you promise me you won't talk to anybody or continue doing this. If I find out you're not obeying, I'll immediately turn this information over to the police. My friend Cal and I will publish the best fucking story you've ever seen—with your mug shot above the fold. Do we have an understanding?"

Walter nodded.

"Good," Aidan said. "And I'm sorry we didn't really get to talk about your good standing on the state's report card. Next time, though. It sounds like such positive news."

After Aidan left the school district building, he drove to the sheriff's sub-station in La Pine and told Briggs to come out to his car.

"This had better be good," the deputy said. "I was hoping to leave by now, so make it quick."

"Where you going?" Aidan asked.

Briggs looked at his suitcase for a moment. "My cabin."

"Since when do you own a cabin? I thought money was tight."

"That's none of your goddam business. Now, what do you have for me?"

Aidan handed him a small thumb drive with all of the photos.

"What the hell is this?" Briggs asked.

Aidan pressed play.

I work for Gabriel. He's been paying me to help supply girls from school to clients...I'm not the pimp's only supplier. A social worker is also involved.

"What the fuck, Aidan?" Briggs asked. "How'd you get this? You're not a deputy. Stop pretending to be one."

"Well, start acting more like one. At least I got some proof for you."

Briggs flipped him off. "How do I know this is even real? A judge could throw this shit out. Seriously, Ade, you've got to be more careful. I don't want you to get hurt."

Briggs motioned to another deputy, who was heading out of the station and getting into his patrol vehicle.

"Niles, come here," Briggs said. "I'd like you to take us for a quick ride-along."

Aidan shook his head.

"Get in the car, Ade," Briggs said. "It's time you see what it's really like to be a deputy so you can understand why it's not as simple as your wannabe, vigilante bullshit."

Niles sped off as soon as Briggs got in the front and Aidan hopped in the back.

"Hang on tight," Niles said. "You're in for a ride."

The deputy swerved through La Pine's few main streets, then tore down the rural region's back roads, spewing a cloud of dust into the air. Niles checked the screen on his Panasonic Toughbook. He looked at the list of runs and locations until Dispatch crackled through the small black Motorola radio on his left shoulder.

"Dispatch to one-eighty."

"This is one-eighty," Niles said.

"We've got a Code four-fifteen."

"Roger that."

Niles turned the car around and hit the gas.

"It's your lucky day," Briggs said as he looked back at Aidan.

"Why, what's a four-fifteen?"

"Noise disturbance."

Aidan rolled his eyes as Briggs laughed and Niles drove into a trailer park. For the next half hour, the deputies interviewed some neighbors yelling at each other about a radio blaring too loud, and then hopped back into the car.

"Now comes the fun part," Niles said. "The paperwork."

"Seriously?" Aidan asked. "You have to write up a report just for that?"

"You bet, and I–"

Dispatch interrupted them.

"Dispatch to one-eighty."

"This is one-eighty."

"We've got a ten-forty-six."

"Roger that," Niles said and then turned to Aidan: "Mental patient."

Niles sped south toward another trailer park. There he interviewed a boy with autism who had allegedly attacked his parents because they threw away his comic books.

Five minutes later, Dispatch crackled again into Niles' radio, alerting him to a complaint about some teens tossing trash off a bridge. "Ade, get back in the car now."

Aidan hadn't even shut the door before Niles gunned it. The deputy hit 60, 70, 80, 90 and then 100 mph on the highway before swerving down a side street that led to the bridge. But by the time they arrived and got out of the car, the teens were nowhere to be found.

"Welcome to our world," Briggs said as he slapped him hard on the back. "You see what we have to deal with all day? La Pine isn't big, but we still get lots of calls about stupid, petty crimes. That's why it's so hard to pursue leads about sex trafficking. Some days we get to bust meth labs, but most of our time is spent dealing with this kind of shit and filling out all that damn paperwork on the computer."

After getting back in the car, Niles took a deep breath. He adjusted the thirteen-pound leather belt on his waist and took a sip of his coffee. He got one bite into his granola bar before he heard the radio again. Another dog complaint.

"Looks like you've got another big assignment," Aidan said.

"Looks like it's time you go cover another parade," Briggs

replied.

After the deputies dropped him back off at the station, Aidan took a long smoke break. Thinking about everything Briggs had said.

Then he drove home, cooked dinner, put Indie to bed and spent the rest of the night with Reina. But as he lay in his own bed with his wife that evening, he couldn't help but think that right now—in Central Oregon—girls were being forced to lie in random beds with men they didn't know.

He just needed a prostitute to help him prove it.

CHAPTER 9

The next day, Camille reminded Zoey that she had to work after school.

Zoey couldn't stand the thought of her sister slaving away one more day for someone who "works for the pimp," as that school administrator had told her. So she decided to tell her sister what she found out about Jacob—and then do something about it.

When they went back to the workshop, that familiar sound of mechanical parts shooting along a conveyer belt greeted the girls. The same men and women still sat in their cell-like cubicles, drawing pictures or playing with dolls in the dull windowless room illuminated only by bulbs. The others continued assembling those parts.

"Where is he?" Zoey asked Camille.

Camille looked over her shoulder and then hung her head to the ground as Jacob approached.

"There you are," the social worker said to her sister. "We've been worried for you, Camille. What happened? Where'd you go?"

Zoey glared at Jacob. "Oh, I think you might know."

"Excuse me?"

"Don't bullshit me. You know exactly what happened."

The vein in Jacob's shaved head began to bulge again. Zoey kept glaring at him. But then the social worker's face calmed. A sick smile even formed on his face as he motioned for a security guard and then turned toward her sister.

"Did something bad happen to you, Camille? You can tell me or our guard. We'll report it right away."

To Zoey's horror, Camille shook her head.

"Well then, Zoey, I suggest you go back to school," Jacob said. "You've caused enough distress for my client today. As you know, Camille has multiple developmental disabilities. She's high functioning, but still has a hard time distinguishing between reality and fantasy."

That sick smile on his face grew even wider.

"As her sister, you of all people should be helping her believe the truth and not encouraging some lies. Mark, can you please escort Zoey out of here?"

As the security guard dragged Zoey out the door, she saw tears form beneath Camille's eyes.

Once Zoey left the workshop, she called Damien.

She had to find out how he could help—if that was even possible. Zoey texted him to meet her at the library. Within a few minutes he showed up and sat down next to her at a table in the back.

For a while they just sat there together. The sound of cell phones and computer games grew louder until Damien finally broke the silence.

"I know you probably don't want to talk about this right now," Damien said. "But like I told you the other day, I came up with an idea that may help us."

Zoey still felt skeptical. Damien pulled a flip phone from his pocket, took a picture of her and set it on the table.

"What's this?" she asked. "Some kind of joke?"

"No," he replied. "It's proof. Proof that you're here in this room. Right now."

Zoey shrugged her shoulders. "So?"

"Nobody can argue with photographic proof," Damien said. "We can use their weapon against them. If we could capture them in the act of pimping—on camera—we'd have enough proof to take down my dad's gang."

"So, why haven't you done that?" Zoey asked.

"Because I've never found someone who was willing to help me stand up to them," Damien replied. "Until I met you."

Zoey looked at the phone on the table. She stared into the small little camera lens. It felt like it was watching her. Waiting. Even now, she shuddered at the thought of receiving another nude or bloody photo.

"So here's the thing," Damien continued. "I know this may sound crazy, but it's our only hope of escaping and finding your mom's killer. I need you to go along with their games for a bit, to pretend like you still want to get those photos back. I know you haven't been to the motel yet, but I'm going to tuck this phone inside a vent."

When Damien finished talking, Zoey just stared at him.

"You actually want me to fuck some random guys?" she asked.

"Of course not, Zoey. I didn't want any of this to happen. But it did. And I'm sorry. But I also know we can get out of this. Even if we catch one client, this could work."

Zoey thought hard for a while. There had to be another way. She considered calling the cops. But then she remembered what Gabriel had said about one of them working for him.

"Couldn't you just catch your own dad in the act?" she asked. "Maybe even talking to his gang?"

"They're too smart for that," Damien replied. "Trust me, I've tried catching Dad before. The last time I did, he gave me that scar."

Zoey handed the flip phone back to Damien.

"I can't do it," she said. "It's too dangerous, especially if your dad really did hire someone to kill our mom. And I barely have the strength to even make it through the day, Damien. I'm so tired. And scared."

"So am I," he replied. "But we can do this."

Damien handed the phone back to Zoey. She picked it up and put it in her pocket.

"Just promise me one thing," she said. "You don't stop helping me until Camille—and every other girl—is free."

CHAPTER 10

The next day, Aidan called the number Ella gave him the night of her death.

"Hello?" asked a tired voice.

"Hi, is this Zoey?"

She didn't answer, so he continued.

"My name's Aidan. I met your mom at the strip club right before she passed away. I'm so sorry about what happened to her, but she gave me your number and wanted me to call you."

He heard a click.

"Damn it," Aidan said as he called Zoey back. The phone went straight to voicemail. He tried a few more times throughout the morning at work. Aidan decided to try once more. This time she answered.

"What the hell do you want?"

"I want to help you and your sister."

"We don't need your help. Mom was the only one who..."

Aidan heard the girl cry.

"Look, I'm so sorry about what they did to your mom, but she made me promise to–"

"Shut the fuck up," Zoey interrupted. "How dare you talk about our mom. Don't ever call us again."

Once Zoey hung up, Aidan grabbed the list of names that Leah had given him. He looked at the lines he had made through their names, crossing them off one by one as they refused to talk to him or Cal.

Zoey and Camille had been their last chance to expose this conspiracy. Aidan started to scratch their names off the list, too. But then he stopped. He had made a promise to the girls' mother.

Suddenly, his phone rang. It was Reina.

"Ade, come home right now," his wife said. "It's Indie. There's blood everywhere. Oh my God, there's so much blood."

Aidan had never sped so fast in his life. He raced through roundabouts and shot past stop signs.

Maybe she just fell.
Maybe she cut herself.
Or maybe someone hurt her.

That last thought made Aidan speed home even faster. After he finally pulled into the driveway, he saw Reina holding Indie. She was covered in blood, but playing with her dolls.

"Babe, what's going on?" Aidan asked. "Is she OK?"

Reina threw her arms around him.

"Thank God you're here," she said. "Indie's fine, but she found this on the front porch and started playing with it."

Reina handed him a Western diamondback rattlesnake. Someone had decapitated it and shoved a note down its neck that read:

Stop now.

"What the hell does that mean?" Reina asked. "What's going on?"

Aidan froze.

"Oh my God," he said. "It's a death threat. From *them.*"

"From who? Ade, what are you talking about? Is this about your story?"

Aidan picked Indie up and held her tight.

"Yeah, but I never thought they'd come here," he said. "I never thought they'd do something like this. Jesus, are you sure Indie is OK?"

"She's fine," Reina said. "I already looked at her. But Ade, who did this?"

Aidan stared at the snake.

"I don't know," he said. "But look, babe, I need you to trust me on this. I can't stop now."

His wife started crying. She took Indie from his arms and glared at him.

"Do you hear yourself talking?" she asked. "You're so obsessed with helping these girls that you're not seeing what's happening to your own wife and daughter. I was so scared when I saw Indie with that thing."

"I know," Aidan said. "So am I. But I need you to let me finish this story. It's the only way to keep you girls safe."

Reina shook her head and walked back into the house without him.

CHAPTER 11

Zoey didn't trust Aidan.

The last thing she needed was another stupid adult to make her life worse. And it got even worse with the next text message from Gabriel:

Meet @ 12am @ Jugs for next client. Bring Camille. Ur working double until we find Walter.

This was it. Her first client since their trip to Seattle.

Zoey lay down on her cot in Josiah's trailer. She was torn. It felt like a scaly insect was crawling around in her brain, cracking her into two distinct halves that grew farther and farther apart. One half was a high school girl named Zoey who wanted to fight back at her pimp and help her sister escape. But the other half, the teenage prostitute, cowered at her captor.

I can't go, she thought. *But you have to.*

Pacing around Josiah's trailer, she tried thinking of anything she could do to get them out of this, to stop her and Camille from going. Zoey began to breathe hard. She could taste thick sweat dripping down her forehead and into her mouth.

I just won't go.
He'll beat you.
I'll run away.
He'll catch you again.
I'll call the cops.
He'll kill me next.

Zoey kept thinking of every possible situation, but nothing helped. The only option that made sense was trying Damien's camera idea. What Gabriel and his gang had used to capture her, she would use to free herself, Camille and every other girl. Finally, the clock struck eleven. No time left.

Zoey glanced at Josiah and his parents. They were now fast asleep in the trailer, snoring loudly next to their own space heater. She took a deep breath and headed outside with Camille, making sure to close the door quietly. A light snow began to fall as they walked along the highway. Each step took her one foot closer to having sex with another man. Another stranger. She just hoped he wouldn't be rough—or at least that the drugs would numb the pain again.

"What's he going to do to Camille?" her sister asked.

Zoey trembled when she heard her sister ask that question. But instead of answering, she told Camille about Damien's idea as they trudged to the truck stop.

Her sister stopped walking. "You can't do that. You'll get caught. That's why Camille couldn't tell the truth the other day at the workshop. She doesn't want to get killed."

Zoey started to answer, but Camille interrupted her.

"Why do you even trust Damien?" Camille said. "His dad's a pimp."

Those words struck Zoey in the gut. Maybe she was wrong. Maybe Damien was setting them up for something even worse.

"You're right," Zoey said. "Damien's dad is a pimp. But he's not. And I think he wants to escape just as much as we do."

The two stopped talking when they saw lights from the strip club. They looked eerie shining down on the lot that sat mostly empty, except for two semis parked in the back. A winter wind blew wisps of snow across the asphalt like white tumbleweed. Camille grabbed Zoey's hand and stepped inside.

Damien was there waiting for them. He led them to a dark booth behind the stage. Zoey wondered if this was where Gabriel did his work. She could imagine the pimp manipulating and intimidating young girls with his clever choice of words. Zoey just hoped it didn't work on her. She had to stay strong.

That's when she saw *him* again. And heard his cane. That fucking cane.

"Hi girls," Gabriel said as he stepped toward them, smoking a cigar. "I'm glad you could meet us tonight."

Camille clutched Zoey's hand beneath the table. Zoey herself started shaking and scratching again.

"First, I'm so sorry again about your mom," the pimp said. "She was such a wonderful woman and one of my best employees. But unfortunately, your mom talked to that photographer. So, someone had to deal with her."

Zoey couldn't tell for sure, but it looked like Gabriel winked at her.

"You sick bastard," Zoey screamed as she shot her middle finger at the pimp. "Did you kill her?"

The pimp remained motionless.

"Calm down, little girl," Gabriel said. "Don't waste your energy on questions like that, because you're never going to find out. You know why? Because the moment you do—hell, if I even so much as catch you trying to snoop around—I'll have the same man kill you and Camille. Even my own son if I find out he's helping you."

Gabriel pointed a pistol at their heads. "Do we have an understanding?"

Zoey and Camille nodded, but Damien stood up and slammed his fist on the table.

"Stop it, Dad. You've done enough to these girls."

The pimp cocked his gun.

"Shut the fuck up, Damien. If you'd waited a little longer, you would've realized there was something else I wanted to talk to them about. I know it's been rough for you girls, so I was hoping to make it up to you with a little gift."

Gabriel handed each of them a giant bag of finely crushed crystal and a wad of cash.

"How much is that?" Damien asked.

"More than you'll ever make," Gabriel said. "This is for each of you from your Daddy. Normally my girls don't get anywhere near this amount, but that film we made in Seattle has brought in a lot of money for us lately, so we figured it was time to celebrate and share some with you."

Zoey had never seen so much cash in her life. But what made her salivate even more was the meth.

"Why are you doing this?" she asked.

"I already told you," Gabriel said. "You've made more than we ever expected. If you keep it up, in another month or two we could all go on a trip somewhere together. Maybe Vegas. There's a lot more cash to make there than in this shithole."

Damien grabbed the sisters' hands and shook his head. But before they could do anything, Gabriel pulled the gifts back.

"How about I give these to you later," the pimp said. "It's time you meet your new friends."

Gabriel led them through a back door of the club and out into the night as a white van with tinted windows rolled toward them. Two figures emerged. Zoey recognized Leah right away. The other woman must have weighed more than 300 pounds. She looked older. And mean.

"Good evening, ladies," Gabriel said. "All right, let's get started. First, give me your cell phones. You know the rules."

The girls handed them over.

"Now, it's time for your new names," the pimp continued. "Zoey, you're Iris. Camille, you're Rose. That's what all the clients will call you. These are your new names. Your new lives. Don't ever use your other ones or there'll be consequences. Got it?"

They agreed.

"Good, now let me introduce you to your new friends," Gabriel said. "You already know Leah—or Ivy, I should say. And this is Jasmine. They're your new family, and they're going to teach you the game tonight on the track. But before we go any farther, here's a little gift for all of you from your Daddy."

This time, Gabriel put the drugs in their hands. Jasmine and Ivy immediately snorted some. Zoey and Camille just stood there.

"You know you want some," the pimp said. "Your bodies must be craving it by now."

Zoey grabbed the bag from Jasmine's hand and snorted a little. Within seconds, her shaking stopped as she felt a warmth and rush of pleasure shoot through her body. She started to take another hit, but Jasmine tried to snatch it from Zoey with her sausage-like thumbs.

"Bitch, gimme some," Jasmine said with a rough, cigarette voice. "You gotta share."

Zoey held on to the bag.

"Oh, shit," Ivy said. "You're fucked."

Jasmine lunged at her like an elephant seal, enveloping her body in folds of fat and tattoos.

"Get off me, you freak," Zoey screamed.

Camille tried to help Zoey, but Jasmine tossed her away.

"Bitch, nobody comes between Jasmine and her crank," she said, flattening Zoey's already tiny body to the ground.

Jasmine started to get up, but then fell back on top of Zoey.

"Shit, I think I'm stuck again," Jasmine said. "Help me up."

By now, Gabriel and Ivy were laughing so hard it looked like they were in pain. After they rolled Jasmine off, Zoey felt like her body had just gone through a press.

"All right," Gabriel said. "I think you bitches are ready to bond."

He handed the van keys to Jasmine, and the four girls sped north to Bend on Highway 97. Nobody talked. They just stared at wisps of snow that slithered across the asphalt like white snakes.

"Daddy always likes to start new girls on the street," Ivy said. "He's old school that way. Plus, the johns here have a lot more money."

Zoey and Camille looked out the backseat window.

"I hope you know that–" Ivy started to say.

"Go to hell," Zoey interrupted.

"Whoa," Jasmine said. "Bitch has got some attitude. I like that."

"Give her time," Ivy said. "Iris will come around eventually."

"Stop calling me that. My name's Zoey. And you're not sorry. You betrayed me and my sister, and now you're taking us to our first trick, so you'd better–"

Before she could continue, Jasmine reached back with her flabby fist and slapped Zoey across the face.

"Your name ain't Zoey no more," Jasmine said. "It's Iris. And your sister's Rose. If we ever hear you say anything different, Daddy's gonna come after you, you hear?"

The sisters nodded.

"A'ight, we're here," Jasmine said, pulling off the highway onto China Hat Road.

The girls stepped out of the white van and onto the dark road that ran perpendicular to the train tracks. The snow had stopped, but the clouds had faded from the sky, turning the high desert into a frozen wasteland. Still feeling good from the meth, Zoey watched as Jasmine and Ivy slid into their sneakers, threw on some black hoodies and started walking down the frozen road that crunched beneath their feet and baggy pants.

Jasmine tossed them each a bag of mushy Twinkies. Apparently that was dinner. Maybe breakfast. Either way, Zoey thought it smelled like moist feet. She didn't dare think about where those Twinkies had been.

"Is that all you're wearing?" Zoey asked.

"What do you mean?" Ivy said.

"I guess I just thought you'd all be wearing a short miniskirt or a tank top or something."

"Here we go again," Jasmine said. "Another Pretty Woman believer. You know how much that Julia Roberts bitch lied in that stupid-ass movie? That ho ain't from the streets. Us bitches know better."

Jasmine looked at Ivy, who smiled in agreement.

"We've got to stay warm, you know?" Jasmine continued. "It's fucking cold out here. Good thing is, most of the time we're in motels now. Either way, the johns don't give a shit. They know we'll take their money. If you wanna walk out here in yo' white trash skirt, go ahead."

The four girls continued walking in silence, black ice cracking beneath their feet, until they stood beneath a rusty old lamppost that flickered in the moonlight. As Zoey looked up and down China Hat Road, she began to wonder if anything was going to happen.

"Where the hell are these guys anyway?" Zoey asked.

"Don't worry," Ivy replied. "They'll start coming soon."

"But it's three in the morning," Zoey said. "Why would any guy want to come out here now?"

"'Cuz they can," Jasmine answered this time. "'Cuz they're sick sons of bitches who just wanna get off. So they tell their girlfriends and wives they're just goin' into work early. I heard this one white boy say he was all lonely, you know, not gettin' any at home 'cuz of the new baby. He started cryin' and shit. I told him to get his sorry ass out of my bed and go back to his white trash wife and kid."

Ivy started laughing. Jasmine took another bite of her Twinkie and then continued.

"I remember this one time I got a guy who was so drunk he actually said he was a pastor. A fuckin' pastor! But he was so nervous and shit he couldn't even get it up, you know? So I just kept teasin' him until he finally left the room cursin'. That was one of my best nights 'cuz..."

Bright headlights appeared in the darkness like two cat eyes creeping toward them.

"A'ight, here we go," Jasmine said.

"What do we do?" Zoey asked, grabbing Camille's coarse hand.

"Just watch the pro," Ivy replied.

Zoey looked on as Jasmine started heading south in the same direction as the car, walking fast enough that she looked like she meant business, but slow enough that it didn't look like she was really going anywhere.

"That's one of the best signals," Ivy said. "You've got to walk like a ho."

Sure enough, the car pulled right up beside Jasmine, who tossed the van keys to Zoey. It was hard to see the man's features, but she was shocked to see a rather good-looking young guy in a suit roll down his window and tell Jasmine to get in the car.

Within five seconds, Jasmine was gone.

"That's it?" Zoey said.

"What were you expecting?" Ivy asked.

"I don't know. Maybe some flirting or a little stripping."

"Oh Iris, you've really got to get this idea out of your head," Ivy said. "Nothing about the game, the life, is sexy. It's not cute. It's not hot. It's just about fucking or getting fucked. The johns already know what they want, and we give it to them because they've got money that keeps Daddy happy and us safe."

Zoey froze beneath the lamppost for another hour, but nobody else came.

"Daddy just texted me," Ivy said. "He wants us to go back to La Pine. I guess a john wants to meet one of you at the motel."

"How do these clients know about us?" Zoey asked.

"Through porn, of course," Ivy replied. "That's the best tool. Daddy posts photos and video on sites like Backpage. He uses those shots they took of you in Seattle and edits them to look like a legit ad. Of course, they're all selling sex."

Zoey cringed at those words as she climbed back into the van. She wondered how many guys even knew what was going on behind their computer screens—or that they were part of this fucking problem.

"I know you hate me," Ivy said. "But there was nothing else I could do. Daddy wanted me to recruit you. I tried disobeying him one time with another girl, and he... Just don't disobey him, OK? You'll regret it."

As Ivy drove, the sisters sat next to each other in the back. The clock on the van showed it was now five in the morning, and they were both cold. Zoey started shaking again. Her teeth chattered. And a splitting headache struck.

While Zoey stared out the tinted windows, she saw moms and dads on their way to work, sipping coffee from Starbucks travel mugs. Some were wearing suits. Others looked like construction workers. For the second time, Zoey felt like she was peering through glass into another world—one she could never re-enter.

An hour later they pulled up to Motel Thrift, near Jugs

Strip Club and Baldy's Truck Stop.

The motel's neon sign flickered in the moonlight, about ready to go dark. It just read "Mote rift." Zoey held Camille's hand as they got out of the van and followed Ivy up the metal stairs to their rooms.

"All right, Iris, this is your room," Ivy said as she pointed to a tan door that had lost most of its paint. "You're in eight fifty-one. Most of the time you'll be here, although sometimes Daddy may have you turn tricks in trucks over at the lot or other random places. Also, don't worry about the motel manager. Daddy's paid him well to keep quiet."

Zoey couldn't believe it. Gabriel had thought of everything.

"Your first client should be up soon," Ivy continued. "Rose, you're next door. That's good, by the way. Most of Daddy's other retards are in the nasty rooms, but he wanted you to have a nicer one. So, stay in there tonight, because another john might come later."

Ivy unlocked their rooms and then walked back down the metal stairs. Camille raced up to Zoey and hugged her.

"Camille can't do this," her sister said.

"Come on," Zoey replied. "Let's go into my room."

The smell of stale cigarettes greeted the girls as they stepped inside Room 851. It was cold. Zoey flipped on the lights to reveal a hard bed covered in stains of God knows what. The bed sat atop a short tan carpet that felt like bristle. A few old paintings of wolves and eagles hung on the walls, staring down at them with accusing eyes.

Zoey looked around the room and saw it. There was the vent, just as Damien had said. She grabbed a wooden chair by the bed and climbed on top of it. Peering into the vent, she saw a small cell phone.

"It's here," Zoey said. "Oh thank God."

She reached into the vent and snatched the phone. As Zoey turned it on, she stared into the black lens of the phone's tiny camera, amazed that this electronic eye could both capture and free someone with one click of a button.

Suddenly, the girls heard the sound of footsteps ascending the stairs.

Clank clank.

"It's OK Camille, you're OK," her sister said, dropping to the floor and curling up into a ball. "It's OK Camille, you're OK."

Zoey grabbed Camille and tried to calm her. "Listen to me. You're going to be fine, but I need you to do everything I say, all right?"

Camille nodded and stood back up. The footsteps were getting closer.

Clank clank. Clank clank.

"Quick, take this phone and hide in the closet," Zoey said. "When he starts to touch me, take your best shot."

"Camille can't do this. She just can't. She isn't strong."

Clank clank. Clank clank. Clank clank.

"Yes you are, Camille. Now come on. We can do this."

Zoey shoved Camille into the closet, turned off the lights and flopped onto the bed. Just then, the door swung open.

"Give it to me hard, bitch," a man said. "I want my money's worth."

She didn't know what to do or say.

"I said I want my money's worth, bitch."

"What do you want?" Zoey asked.

"Take your panties off and turn around. I don't got all day."

Piece by piece, Zoey started removing her clothes. Her fingers trembled with each button. Her heart thumped, pumping blood violently through her veins.

Come on, Camille. You can do it.

The man stepped closer. Stumbled on top of her. Now she could hear his heavy breathing. Now she could smell the whiskey in his mouth.

Please, Camille. Don't let him hurt me.

The closet door remained closed as Zoey finally removed her panties. She was now completely exposed, her bare butt facing upward. She could hear the man's pants unzip.

Please, Camille.

"Take that, you bastard," Camille shouted as she shot flashes of light into the darkness of the room.

"What the hell?" the man said, jumping in surprise. "Who the fuck is this bitch?"

"It's Camille, bitch. And Camille's your worst nightmare if you don't get out of here in ten seconds."

Zoey couldn't believe what she was hearing. Each time Camille took another shot, the man tried to see her. But that proved impossible without the lights on.

"I don't believe you," the man said as he stepped toward her. "You bitches are fucked."

"No, you're fucked," Zoey said as she jumped off the bed. "I swear to God, if you take one more step toward my sister I'll blow your brains out. And if you tell anyone—including our pimp—about what happened tonight, everyone will see these photos of you. I know your family and friends. I'm sure they'd be pretty shocked to hear you're spending the next decade in prison for raping a teen."

Zoey could hear the man breathing harder. She knew he

was trying to see whether she really had a gun, but it was too dark. The room became so silent it felt suffocating.

"Stupid bitches. I want my money back."

"You're not getting anything back," Zoey said. "Except your clothes, and you'd better put those on now before I start shooting."

Grumbling, the man tossed on his shirt. Pulled up his pants. And then left. He slammed the door behind him.

"You did it," Zoey said.

She put her own clothes back on and then raced up to Camille. Both girls held each other in the dark as they tried to comprehend what had just happened.

Finally, Zoey calmed down enough to speak. "I've never heard you talk like that before, Camille. You never swear."

"Camille used to swear all the time when Jacob stopped taking her on outings," her sister said. "But every now and then, Camille's Hulk comes back."

Zoey laughed. "Well, you should use your Hulk more often. Did you see that guy's face? It looked whiter than his ass."

The sisters sat next to each other on the bed as they started looking through their photos. But whatever smiles they had faded when they stared at each shot.

"Oh no," Zoey said. "These won't work."

"Are you sure?" Camille asked.

Zoey nodded. Each picture was so blurred you couldn't even see the faces.

"Camille's sorry," her sister said.

"It's not your fault. We just have to catch another client. But first, we've got to get back to Jo's trailer. His mom's going to freak out if we're not there when she wakes up."

The girls grabbed their clothes and the money the man had

left them. Then they raced out the door and onto the highway. While they walked home, Zoey kept looking up at the moon that peered down on them through the pines with its ghost-like face. It felt like it was staring at them. Accusing them. Exposing them.

Once the sisters got back to the trailer, they fell asleep for only a few minutes until Marge woke them up. As they got ready to leave for school, Josiah put his hand on Zoey's shoulder.

"Hey Zo," Josiah said. "You OK? You and Camille seem pretty tired this morning."

After being called Iris so many times last night, the name Zoey sounded distant, like something out of a dream she could barely remember.

"I'm fine," Zoey lied. "Just couldn't sleep much last night. Kept thinking about Mom."

Josiah nodded.

"I get it," he said. "Hey, how about we get some Dairy Queen after school sometime this week? It's been forever."

Zoey agreed, wondering if she could ever tell Josiah what she was going through.

CHAPTER 12

Aidan couldn't focus at work.

Reina's words still weighed on his mind, so after touching base with Mitch on all of his photo assignments, he got permission to work from home the rest of the day.

Aidan drove back to their house, parked his Subaru, cleaned the dashboard, wiped down his camera lens and walked inside just as it started to snow again. Aidan plopped down on the couch to take a nap before Reina left her copywriting job to pick Indie up and come home. He tried to sleep, but couldn't. The sight of that snake kept creeping back into his mind.

He had to be more careful. But he couldn't give up on this story.

Boiling a pot of water, Aidan made a cup of dark coffee with their French press. He tried reading the lead article in today's paper, but found himself going over the same paragraph again and again. It had something to do with the city wrangling over their new logo. What a stupid story. And waste of time.

Finally, Aidan threw the paper in the recycle bin and fired up his laptop. He spent a few minutes looking for newspaper jobs in Seattle. As usual, nobody was hiring.

Aidan decided to research Gabriel Lester. Briggs was right—Gabriel had a clever alibi in the strip club. The only documents Aidan could find proved that he was just a wealthy businessman and philanthropist.

He spent a few more minutes researching Gabriel and then turned to Jacob Combs, the social worker with the local board of developmental disabilities that the school administrator had mentioned. Aidan learned from public records that Jacob had come to the region in 2009 after suddenly leaving a small county board in Ohio. Local news stories at the time had raised questions of sexual abuse and disciplinary action, but Jacob was never charged with a crime.

After researching Jacob a little more, Aidan decided to turn his attention to sex trafficking as a whole. He confirmed from official records that what Briggs had told him at the pub was true; forced labor and human trafficking was a multi-billion dollar business, enslaving millions of people worldwide. It was modern day slavery.

But what Aidan just couldn't believe was how much trafficking appeared to be a growing problem in America, too. Even Oregon. Although pimps were capturing women from distant places such as Thailand, they were also coercing thousands of victims in the United States—and they were doing that with sophisticated online tools like Backpage.com.

Just out of curiosity, Aidan went to Bend's Backpage website and looked under the "adult" section. What he saw shocked him. There were links to "adult jobs," "body rubs," "dom & fetish" and more. Every category he clicked on flashed half-naked photos of women wearing string bikinis or lingerie, offering all types of service:

> *PARTY GIRL real pic WHITE GIRL 4 U.*
> *Big booty, slim waist, great taste.* ☺
> *Double Your Pleasure with Vicki & Shannon.*
> *Sexy White Chocolate.*
> *Exotic Playmate Last Night in Town!!!!*
> *Delicious Petite Blonde Barbie.*

One of the links directed him to a photo of a young woman spread-eagle on a bed.

If it wasn't for his wife's past, Aidan probably wouldn't care about looking at pictures like these. But he could hear Reina in the back of his mind, telling him when they were dating that she couldn't marry another man who looked at porn because her last husband got arrested for child pornography. Aidan never told her about his past, probably out of shame or embarrassment. Maybe both.

Aidan clicked off that page and continued researching. But the image of that hot woman kept brewing in his mind as he searched on Google, urging him to take another peek. He decided to go back and find that photo again. Then he saw how many other options were available:

> *Barely legal lesbians!!!* read one ad. *Just turned 18! Hot XXX young girls lick each other now!!!*

His finger trembled. That sickening, nervous feeling grew inside him again.

I deserve this.
No you don't.
I'll just take a quick peek.
Reina will catch you.
I'll hide the history.
She'd kill me.

Aidan slammed his laptop shut and called Cal. "Let's ride."

"Now? But I've still got to file my story. And it's going to get dark soon."

"Then hurry up and finish it. I just gave Mitch my weather photo. Meet me at Phil's Trailhead in thirty minutes."

———

Once Aidan got to the trail, he was relieved to see no other cars or people.

It was cold, but at least the ground wasn't wet. Before him lay an open dirt road that wound deep into a forest filled with pillars of ponderosa pines. He loved that sight. He could disappear into that trail, becoming one with the bike as it crunched rocks beneath his feet. It was in these woods that he felt most at peace with the world. His problems became like pebbles flattened by mountain tires.

The coarse sound of Cal's beater shook Aidan from his musings. He could have sworn he saw a few jackrabbits scurry away into the bitterbrush.

"You're late," Aidan said.

Cal didn't seem to care; he was too focused on his new Cannondale bike. "Let's do this."

The two friends hopped on their bikes and tore through the first stretch of trail. Tree branches whipped past their faces like gnarled fingers as they sped up and down the endless mounds of dirt that threatened to dump them into the nearby river. But Aidan and Cal had ridden this trail so many times they knew every turn by heart. They easily hopped over the first jump, landing solidly on the red dirt that stained their pedals.

"Ready for the big one?" Cal yelled to Aidan who trailed right behind him.

Within seconds, Cal flew over a giant mound that shot him clear across a puddle of mud. Aidan followed him, but his front spokes snagged a low-lying root that locked his tire, jammed his bike and hurled him face down into the muck below.

Cal stared at his friend. Then he burst into laughter.

"Shit," Aidan muttered. "Are you kidding me? Did that really just happen?"

Cal pulled Aidan out of the mud, amazed that he wasn't bruised or bleeding. The bike was another story. The front tire was twisted, and the back wouldn't even spin.

"Well, I guess you know what to get me for Christmas," Aidan said.

He moved his bike under a tree with Cal's help and sat down on the ground to take a break. The two split a granola bar and shared water from a Nalgene bottle. Neither spoke for a while.

"Can I ask you something?" Aidan finally said. "It's kind of personal."

"Sure, anything."

Aidan shifted on the ground.

"I don't even know why I'm talking to you about this," he said. "But do you think it's bad to look at porn?"

Cal's eyes narrowed. "Why?"

"Well, I used to look at porn all the time before I met Reina," Aidan said. "I was pretty obsessed. Almost as much as my cleaning and organizing. Anyway, I saw some today for the first time in ages while researching this whole sex trafficking thing. Most of the girls had clothes on, but some of them were basically nude. And really young."

Aidan felt embarrassed.

"I know I'm not hurting anybody," he continued. "To be honest, I don't even know why I'm telling you. It's just that I always feel, I don't know..."

"Guilty?" Cal asked.

"No," Aidan replied. "Of course not. What the hell does that mean anyway? I've never cheated on my wife. I love my daughter. I only drink fair trade coffee. Shit, even my cigarettes are organic. It's the people I photograph in court who are fucking guilty—the goddam pedophiles and rapists."

Cal nodded.

"I get it, bro," he said. "Look, I'm just trying to help. You're a great friend, Ade, and I just don't want to see you go through the same hell I did."

Aidan took a sip from his Nalgene bottle and stared at his friend. "What are you talking about?"

"It's getting dark," he said. "We should go soon."

Aidan felt a jabbing pain in his stomach. He looked down and saw a small gash on his side where he knew a pine branch had snagged him right before the crash. A little bit of blood seeped from his cut. Cal handed him a bandage from his pack.

"How the hell are we friends?" Aidan asked.

"What do you mean?"

"We're not anything alike. I was raised by atheists. You grew up in a Bible-thumping family that doesn't drink, which I still don't understand by the way. Didn't Jesus himself turn water into wine?"

"Oh, yeah," Cal said. "He drank wine, went to parties— even hung out with prostitutes. But a lot of Christians today like to forget those facts. Makes Jesus seem a little too edgy."

Aidan stared at his Nalgene bottle. "Well, I sure wish Jesus could turn my water into wine right now. This granola bar tastes like shit."

The two friends laughed, packed up their gear and headed back to the car.

On the way home, Aidan stopped by a local market to get Reina some flowers.

Then he grabbed every bottle of cleaning solution he could find. Room by room, he scrubbed every window. Every counter. And every beam of wood in their home. They only had a three-bedroom house, but it still took more than an hour.

Reina hadn't asked him to clean, but he wanted to show her his love. Plus, Aidan always felt better about himself whenever he cleaned. It satisfied his OCD. And it made him feel in control no matter how much was going on around him. Aidan didn't believe in heaven or any of that bullshit, but if he had a soul, Comet would clean it.

Soon, the smell of raw chemicals began to gnaw at his stomach and make him feel nauseous. His glasses started to fog from sweat. Aidan heard his wife and daughter pulling into the garage. He began scrubbing the floors again, this time with even more of a vengeance.

"Honey, we're home," Reina said as Indie ran up to her dad and shoved a bag of jellybeans into his face.

"Here, Daddy. Eat this one."

Aidan plopped a yellow bean into his mouth and then spit it out. Indie giggled.

"That one's booger," she squealed and ran away.

"Come here," Aidan said as he chased her into the kitchen where Reina had already started unpacking the groceries. He strode right past Reina to grab the rest of the bags from her car.

"Hi, honey," she said. "Thanks for cleaning. Looks great. How was your day?"

Aidan pretended not to hear her. When he returned with the groceries, she asked him again.

"Fine," was all he could muster.

"Ade, you OK?" she asked.

"Yeah, sorry, I'm just tired and hungry. I think those chemicals went to my head."

Aidan kissed his wife and then devoted the rest of the evening to spending time with his wife and daughter. He decided to make a fire and some steaming cups of hot chocolate as they watched *The Muppet Christmas Carol* together. He poured a little bit of bourbon into his own cup.

In the back of his mind, Aidan kept thinking about what Cal had said—and how his wife would feel if she caught him.

CHAPTER 13

The next morning, Zoey felt exhausted as she and Camille walked with Josiah through the doors of South County High.

But for the first time since the party that started everything, she also felt hopeful. Like they could survive. They just needed to catch another client.

Then Zoey opened her locker.

She screamed and lurched back at the sight of a rattlesnake. But as Zoey looked closer, she saw that someone had cut off its head and crammed a note down its neck that read:

Stop now.

Whatever hope she had died. It had to be a death threat. From *him*.

Zoey looked around. Thank God, most people had already

left for class, including Josiah and Camille. A couple kids she didn't know looked at her like she was crazy and whispered to each other, but they hadn't seen the snake. So Zoey grabbed it. Shoved the carcass into her backpack. And bolted out the door.

She didn't know where she was going. But Zoey didn't care. She just ran. And ran. And ran. Maybe she'd hitchhike to Eugene. Or Portland. Hell, maybe even San Francisco. Zoey just couldn't take it anymore. She had to get away from him. From his gang. From this whole fucking town.

Zoey only made it a few minutes until the sound of an engine stopped her. She glanced behind her and saw a black car, but couldn't identify the driver. Zoey ran harder. The car picked up the pace, following her from a distance. She took a sudden left turn through a parking lot. So did the car.

Finally, Zoey stopped. She couldn't tell who this person was, but it didn't matter anymore. She sank into the snow, exhausted. After catching her breath, Zoey reached into her backpack, grabbed the dead snake and flung it toward the car.

"Fuck you," she screamed. "Fuck all of you."

By the time Zoey made it back to school, Mr. Brookstone was already halfway through his class.

He nodded to her as he asked everyone to turn in their homework assignment. They were supposed to write a one-page report on the first few chapters from *The Scarlet Pimpernel*. But Zoey had failed. Again. Just like with *Uncle Tom's Cabin*, she had actually wanted to read *The Scarlet Pimpernel*. But she had only made it through a few pages.

"Let's start with an easy question," Mr. Brookstone said. "Who can tell me why the hero, Sir Percy, left behind cards with that flower on them whenever he rescued innocent people sentenced to death by the guillotine?"

A boy in the back raised his hand. "It was his secret symbol, his way of showing the bad guys who he was, and that they'd better watch out. Kind of like Batman."

People started laughing, but Mr. Brookstone cut them off.

"Good job, Brice. You're right. Sir Percy used this flower as a symbol of freedom. It was his way of promising to rescue innocent people as they climbed the steps to death…"

Zoey's mind started wandering again. She flipped through the book and came across a passage someone else had underlined:

The rest is silence, silence and joy for those who had endured so much suffering—yet found at last a great and lasting happiness.

Zoey stopped reading. Images of that snake came back into her mind as she tried to process what it meant.

Was the hit man here?
Was he watching her right now?
Had he seen them taking photos?

"Zoey?" Mr. Brookstone said. "Are you OK? It's time to leave."

She came back from her thoughts to class and realized that everyone had left. "Sorry, I'm just…"

"Don't apologize," Mr. Brookstone said. "But as your teacher, Zoey, I have to ask—are you sure you're doing fine? You and

Camille always look exhausted, and you were late today. What's going on?"

This was it. The loophole. A way out. Zoey couldn't believe she hadn't thought of the idea before. She could just tell Mr. Brookstone everything and have him help them. Surely, the pimp didn't know all of her teachers.

But then Zoey remembered the snake. Her heart sank. If the killer had found a way into her school and locker, surely he'd find out if she was working with a teacher. So once again, she lied. Pretended that everything was fine during the day before heading out into the darkness of the night.

"I'm really sorry," Zoey said. "To be honest, some days I can't even get out of bed. I just lie still, thinking of Mom. That's what's been going on. But that's no excuse."

Mr. Brookstone sighed. "I'm sorry, Zoey. I didn't mean to make you upset."

After talking for a few more minutes, Zoey walked out of the room. She went to the next class, but fell asleep. After the last bell rang, Zoey dragged herself outside like a zombie. More than anything else, she just wanted a good night's sleep for once.

Then Josiah showed up. "Ready for some ice cream?"

Zoey sighed. The two walked in silence toward Dairy Queen, ordered their usual Midnight Truffle Blizzards and then sat down in a booth by the back.

"I know what's going on," Josiah said after taking a break from his ice cream. "I can understand why you won't tell me, but I just wanted to let you know that I'll still like you, no matter what."

Zoey searched his eyes, wondering how he had found out—and how he could ever forgive her.

"A lot of my friends have gotten into crank," Josiah said.

"Trust me, you're not the first. But you're better than that. I know you are."

She didn't know whether to feel relieved or saddened. Zoey didn't want Josiah to learn the truth for fear of him getting hurt by Gabriel's gang, but she also craved for him to know her. The real girl. And not reject her.

"Jo, I'm not who you think–"

"You don't need to say anything," Josiah interrupted. "I understand, and I've forgiven you. Just promise me you'll stop and try to get some help."

Zoey stared at her ice cream melting down the side of its cup. For the first time, Josiah reached across the table and held her hand. She lurched back.

"Don't touch me," Zoey said. "What're you doing?"

"I just wanted to show you how much I love you."

Zoey cringed at those words. "Don't say that. You don't love me. You can't. You don't know who I am."

"Of course I do. Zoey, we've known each other since we were kids. But you've got to let me keep on knowing you."

Zoey stood up. "I just can't let you do that anymore."

She tightened the hoodie over her head and walked out the door as her phone vibrated with another text:

Meet now. 2 clients.

Zoey couldn't believe this was happening. It was still daylight. She had thought the pimp would only want her and Camille to meet at the motel once a week or so. But he wanted them there now—with two johns. Zoey knew it was only a matter of time before that number grew and excuses to Josiah ran out. She sent Jo a quick text and said that she was going to study with Camille again.

"What do they want Camille to do this time?" her sister asked as they walked to the motel. "Camille can't keep making excuses forever."

"I know," Zoey said. "We just have to get one good photo. Make sure you stand still this time while taking the pictures."

"Camille's getting worried. She could get caught—and hurt."

Zoey grabbed her sister's hand as they walked to the motel and up the steps to their rooms.

"How'd it go last night?" Ivy asked.

Zoey felt her stomach tighten. She stared at Ivy, wondering if she knew anything.

"Fine," Zoey replied as Camille nodded in agreement.

"Good, here you go," Ivy said as she unlocked Room 851. "The johns should be up soon. I don't know if Daddy told you, but there are two clients this time. They want to do both of you, so I'm just going to put you in the same room. We're charging double."

After Ivy left, the girls walked into the room and looked around. Nothing had changed. Not even the vent. Zoey reached inside and grabbed the phone. Still working.

For a moment, Zoey thought about going through with their plan. But then she remembered the snake. And the note. And the car. And the fact that the killer might be watching them right now.

"Fuck it," Zoey said. "This whole idea is stupid. I'm calling the cops. We should've done that a long time ago."

"Don't do it," her sister said. "Gabriel said a cop works for him. And that he'd kill you and Camille."

Zoey knew the risk. But she had to take a chance. She dialed 911 and told the operator everything. Then they waited. And waited. And waited. Only a few minutes passed before they heard a car pull up and someone start climbing the stairs, but it felt like forever.

Clank clank.

"This is it," Zoey said. "We're free."

"Camille's scared. What if it's not a cop?"

Clank clank. Clank clank.

"It's got to be. Trust me."

Clank clank. Clank clank. Clank clank.

A sheriff's deputy broke through the door.

"Oh thank God," Zoey said. "Please, you've got to help us."

A big man with a buzzed head and huge arms walked through the door. He looked more like a bodybuilder than a deputy, but that made Zoey sigh even more with relief. He could definitely protect them from their pimp.

"My name's Briggs," the man said. "I just heard about your call from Dispatch. I'm here to help you. But first, give me your phone."

Zoey stared at the deputy. "Excuse me?"

Briggs stepped closer to her and Camille. The man's right hand gripped his heavy leather belt, which held a gun, baton, cuffs and mace.

"You heard me," the deputy said. "Give me the phone now or I'll kill you—just like your fucking whore of a mom."

Zoey's heart sank. Camille dropped to the floor and started shrieking as Damien raced into the room.

"Leave her alone," Damien said. "I set them up to this."

"Back the fuck up," Briggs said. "You've caused enough trouble for your dad."

"You don't need to do this."

The deputy snatched the phone from Camille's hand and called Gabriel with it. Then he smashed it with his baton. The lens shattered. Zoey stared at the phone on the ground, their only hope of freedom scattered across the carpet. Before they could do anything, Gabriel stepped into the room.

"I'll take it from here, Briggs," Gabriel said. "So, I hear you girls have been pretty busy. Taking pictures. Calling the cops. That true?"

Nobody spoke.

"I said, is that true?"

Zoey looked at Damien and Camille, who both kept their eyes glued to the carpet.

"Fine," the pimp said. "It seems like I haven't done a good enough job breaking you girls in yet. So let's try something else."

Slowly, Gabriel took off his black leather jacket and slicked back his white hair.

Then he grabbed Camille by the hair, dragged her to the bed and started beating her with his cane. Briggs watched from a distance. Smiling. Laughing.

"Stop," Zoey said. "Please, don't touch my sister. You can... touch me instead."

The pimp shoved Camille to the ground and tossed Zoey onto the bed. Damien tried racing up to her, but Gabriel aimed a gun at his son's head.

"Back off, boy," the pimp said. "This time, you can't help her. She's mine now."

Zoey closed her eyes. She could feel the pimp pull down her jeans and rip off her panties. As Gabriel touched her, Zoey tried recalling her favorite memory. She could hear Damien and

Camille screaming, but slowly their voices became quieter and the sound of her mom singing grew louder.

This little light of mine.

Zoey felt the cane down below, touching the top of her skin. The wood was coarse and rough. Her legs trembled.

I'm gonna let it shine.

Zoey felt the cane push inside her. The wood was sharp and hard. Her whole body shook.

Let it shine. Let it shine. Let it shine.

Right when Zoey's mind was about to go dark, Gabriel stopped.

"That should be enough," the pimp said. "I have to say, I underestimated you. None of my girls have ever tried defying me like you did. But if you ever try calling the cops or running away again, we'll fucking kill you."

Zoey saw spots in her eyes. She couldn't take much more.

"Unfortunately, this just means you're going to have to make up for lost time," Gabriel continued. "At least you're finally stretched out."

The last thing Zoey remembered was the pimp ripping the cane out of her body and bashing her in the head with it.

Hours later, Zoey awoke and retched all over her bedspread.

Racing to the bathroom, she collapsed to the ground as a sharp pain stabbed between her legs. She crawled the remaining feet to the tub and threw herself in. As the water began to pour over her limp body, she saw it turn crimson beneath her crotch. Zoey sobbed for more than five minutes and then closed her eyes.

She could still see their faces. Not one. Or two. But fourteen. She remembered every one of them. The old man's wet, sweaty skin. The young man's dull, drunken eyes. And the girl's breath that smelled like shellfish. There could have been more. But after that fourteenth man with the whips, Zoey passed out.

Despite what had happened last night, the shower was still her sanctuary. Nobody could touch her here. She lay down on her back and stared into the mist of the water that sprinkled her body, but didn't make her feel clean.

In fact, Zoey had never felt so dirty in her life. She had always wanted her first time to be special, with someone she loved. Now that would never happen. More than a dozen men had stolen that special part from her.

An hour later, Zoey dried off. She stared into the bathroom mirror and recoiled at the stranger. This person appeared old and haggard. The face was so thin, and the arms were now covered in scratch marks from craving more crystal. Even the scar beneath her left eye appeared extra raw this morning, as if the sex last night had somehow deepened the wound. It looked like she was already becoming more like Iris and less like Zoey.

As she started to put her clothes back on, Zoey remembered the razor she had put in her backpack. Just in case. Her whole body was in pain, but maybe it would give her some relief again. So she grabbed the blade and touched it to her wrist.

Zoey started to make a cut, but then remembered Camille.

She couldn't believe she had forgotten about her. Gabriel must have taken Camille to her own room last night. After Zoey wrapped a towel around her wrist to stop the bleeding, she raced back into the bedroom and stared in disbelief at the alarm clock. It was almost time for school.

Zoey grabbed her clothes, limped out of the room and banged on her sister's door. Nobody answered. She pounded again.

"Come on, Camille. It's me. We've got to get back home."

She knocked again, this time harder. "Look, Camille, I know those men hurt you last night. They hurt me, too. But we've got to get back."

The door creaked open and Zoey could see one eye peeking out.

"It's not OK," Camille said. "You're not OK."

"I know," Zoey replied as she opened the door and hugged her.

The sisters grabbed their clothes and started walking back in silence. They moved slowly, each step another stab between their legs from the pain of last night. The snow had finally stopped, but harsh winds from the Cascades whipped their faces raw. Zoey tried hiding in her hoodie, though she still felt the icy air cut her nose and eyes. Not even her steel-toed boots could keep out the cold.

All of a sudden, Camille dropped to the ground. Zoey tried grabbing her hand, but Camille shrieked in pain as she pulled back. Zoey looked at her hands and saw blood.

"What's wrong, Camille? Let me see your hands."

Camille didn't budge.

"Come on, let me see them."

Shaking, Camille took her hands out of her pockets and held them up. They looked like they were on fire. The skin had cracked all over, creating spider webs of blood from her fingernails to her wrists. Between her fingers, the flesh had peeled off.

"What'd you do?" Zoey asked.

"Camille tried cleaning herself with burning water," her sister said. "But he just wouldn't go away. He's still on her skin. He's all over. And Camille can't get him off. She tried washing all night to make her skin white as snow so she could be a pure princess like Snow White. But he's still there."

Reaching beneath her shirt, Camille started scratching as hard as she could with her long fingernails.

"Stop it," Zoey said. "You're going to hurt yourself."

"He's everywhere. Camille can still smell him. Must cut him off."

"No, you're going to cut yourself even worse. Stop it, Camille. Stop!"

Zoey grabbed her sister's hands, but she yanked them back and started screaming again in pain. Too tired to argue anymore, Zoey just sat down on the ground next to Camille and wrapped her arm around her. Camille's disabilities already made it hard for her to deal with stress and changes in routine—let alone all of this. She didn't know how much more her sister could take.

If Aidan couldn't help them now, nobody could.

CHAPTER 14

Aidan couldn't sleep.

As he lay in bed next to Reina, he kept thinking about his conversation with Cal the other day. He could hear Reina snoring, and Indie had fallen asleep hours ago. A sudden urge and feeling of excitement shot through his stomach.

Nobody would know.

Aidan grabbed a pair of boxers and snuck into his office to fire up the laptop. He found that site again and couldn't believe how many options there were and what he could buy. Photos. Phone sex. Web-cam sex. Joint masturbation. Several times, he started feeling guilty when he thought of his wife. He went back to that one ad:

Barely legal lesbians!!! Just turned 18! Hot XXX young girls lick each other now!!!

His finger trembled again. That sick, nervous feeling crept back. And he decided to click on the first girl's picture with his mouse, peering at her through his glasses.

Click.

He looked at the second girl.

Click.

He looked at two girls together.

Click.

"Daddy, what're you watching?" someone asked.

To Aidan's surprise, his daughter Indie stood right behind him.

"I'm sorry," he said, trying to click off of the screen that only produced more explicit and graphic pop-ups. "What do you need, baby girl?"

"I just wanted some water."

He didn't know what to do.

"Indie, is that you?" he heard Reina say from the other room. "What time is it? You're supposed to be sleeping."

Aidan kept clicking, but the pop-ups wouldn't stop. Right as he was about to slam the computer shut, Reina walked into the room. She saw the screen.

"How could you?" his wife asked.

He didn't know what to say.

"Ade, how could you do this?"

Aidan hung his head. He looked at Indie, who kept glancing back and forth between them with a sad and confused look on her little face.

"I'm sorry," he said. "I don't know..."

He tried to explain. But each time, it made the situation worse. And each time, Reina grew more and more upset.

"How about I sleep at Cal's house tonight?" Aidan finally said. "Let's talk more tomorrow."

He grabbed his clothes, flipped off the lights and headed out into the dark.

———————

Aidan knocked on Cal's door.

He must've been fast asleep, because it took a few more knocks before his friend appeared wearing his usual slippers, white long johns and that hideous fur coat.

"Ade, what're you doing here?" Cal asked. "And where's your jacket? It must be ten degrees outside."

"We had a fight," Aidan said. "Can I crash here?"

Cal let him inside their house and down to his man cave. Then his friend tossed a log onto a dying fire that now only glowed with a few embers. Cal lit his briar pipe and poured a pint of beer for both of them. His fiery-red beard looked extra bright next to the flames.

"What the hell is this?" Aidan asked, taking the opportunity to whip out another cigarette.

"My home brew. It's a winter ale. Just finished the batch."

Aidan rolled his eyes. "Why am I not surprised?"

"There's a smile. Come on, bro, tell me what happened with you and Reina."

Aidan took off his glasses and hung his head in his tired hands, listening to the fire crackle as he pulled on his black hair.

"She caught me looking at porn," he said. "Indie, too."

Cal sighed. "I'm sorry, bro."

"I didn't think it'd be that big of a deal," Aidan said. "The girls are eighteen, so they're legal. And again, it's not like I'm hurting anyone. Well, maybe Reina. Her ex had a history with child porn, so I know she hates it. And then there's Indie. God, the way she looked at me with her little eyes still burns my head."

For a while, Aidan just stared into the fire. Then he looked at Cal. "But you wouldn't understand. You're a Christian."

Cal took another swig of beer.

"Yeah, but that doesn't mean I'm perfect, Ade. That's what I was trying to tell you the other day. I used to look at porn all the time. Started before we got married. At first, I thought it'd get better with marriage. And it did. For a while. But I started wanting it again. And before I knew it, I was sneaking out of bed—after we had sex—to look at porn. It's an addiction, bro. Fucking slavery."

Aidan shook his head. "I don't believe you. You guys always seem so good together."

"I'm serious, bro," Cal said. "One day my wife actually caught me. Almost killed our marriage. I realized that it doesn't matter if you're a pimp selling girls or just a guy who likes to look at them. We're all fucked up. We're all part of this problem. The question is—do you even give a shit?"

For a while, Aidan didn't say anything. He just stared at the embers, watching as Cal stoked the fire. Then he shook his head again.

"I don't believe that, Cal. There's a huge difference between me and those guys. I mean, I wasn't out there screwing some underage girl–"

Cal stood up and interrupted him.

"You're still missing the point, Ade. Think about those girls we tried talking to at school for our story. Most of them were seventeen, right? But those girls your wife caught you looking at are just eighteen. Why does a year somehow make it suddenly right for you to look at them, even if it is technically legal? Sure, they're just images, but there's a real girl behind the computer screen—somebody's daughter."

Aidan groaned. "I feel like shit."

"It's called being human, bro," Cal said. "You're not the first person to struggle with this. In fact, you could be any guy. But I can help you. I've been through this before with my wife. Just give her time."

Cal poured Aidan some more beer.

"Maybe this'll cheer you up," he said. "Then let's get some sleep. We've got a huge story to finish."

THE
FLASH

CHAPTER 1

Marge was waiting outside for Zoey and Camille when they finally got back to the trailer.

"Hey girls," she said. "Where've you been?"

This time, Zoey couldn't think of an excuse that would work, so she just remained silent. So did Camille.

"It's OK," Marge added. "I don't need to know, but I do want you girls to go on a drive with me. I've already called you off from school today."

The three got into Marge's old minivan and started heading south along Highway 97. In less than a minute they were out of La Pine. Zoey forgot how fast it took to put this God-forsaken town in the rearview mirror. And yet, most days it felt impossible to escape.

But once Marge passed Michael Road and entered the Deschutes National Forest, Zoey felt like she could breathe again for the first time. It was as if the pine trees hid her in that forest, protecting them from the outside world. The girls continued driving in silence until they reached Highway 138. Marge turned right and then headed south again.

"Where we going?" Zoey asked.

"You'll see, dear," Marge said with a smile.

After a little longer, Zoey saw a sign for Crater Lake. Marge drove to the main entrance. Despite the cold, there were still a few hardy travelers who had pulled off from the highway to see the lake. Zoey had heard about this place so many times, but their mom never had enough gas to take them there. Once they made it to the main ridge, Zoey couldn't believe her eyes.

She had never seen such deep, pure or clear water. It was smooth as glass, contrasting sharply with the jagged cliffs that shot up from the lake almost 2,000 feet high. But what stood out to Zoey most was the silence. Aside from the wind, she heard nothing.

"Beautiful, isn't it?" Marge asked. "Sometimes I can't believe that something so peaceful had such a violent past. It used to be a volcano, you know."

As Zoey looked down from the ridge, it struck her that she could escape. Right here. Right now. She'd just have to jump. The pimp, her mom's death—even the pain from last night—would all just disappear. Forever. Zoey inched closer to the edge, but Marge grabbed her hand.

"Be careful," Marge said. "You could slip."

Zoey sighed.

"My own mom used to take me here," Marge said. "That was a long time ago, back when I was your age—back when I used to cut myself and do crank."

The girls looked at Marge in shock.

"What?" Zoey asked. "I don't believe you."

Marge smiled.

"It's true," she replied. "I used to be really depressed. Still am sometimes today. But you know what helped? It was when my mom took me here and showed me this water and how peaceful it looked. She said I could be like that too someday."

Marge looked at the water for a while and then continued.

"Now, I don't know what all you girls are dealing with. Lord knows you've been through hell with your mom dying. But I know you've been cutting and sneaking out at night to do drugs—and that's no way to deal with it."

Zoey started to say something, but Marge interrupted her.

"I could try to stop you, Zoey. I could keep watch outside the trailer all night and force you girls to stay inside. But at the end of the day, that won't work. I know, because it didn't work for me when my mom tried that. The only way you're going to be able to survive this is by keeping hope."

Zoey and Camille started crying. Marge put her arms around both of the girls and held them tight.

———

When they got back from the crater, Zoey decided to tell Damien about Aidan and how he had promised to help them.

Zoey couldn't risk getting picked up by Damien in front of Josiah's trailer, so she texted Damien to meet her at the Red Rooster Coffee House in La Pine.

She only made it a few steps before Josiah stopped her.

"I wanted to apologize," he said.

"For what?" Zoey asked.

"I shouldn't have said I loved you."

She blushed. Zoey both loved and hated the way Josiah looked at her with those eyes full of concern. She knew he wanted to help her, but so had her mom. And the last thing she needed was another reason for the pimp to retaliate against someone else she cared for.

Zoey gave him a hug. "It's OK, Jo. I shouldn't have walked out on you like that." She kept holding him. His body felt warm and comforting pressed up against hers, especially with his old flannel shirt. Finally, she pulled away. "All right, Jo, I'm going for a walk. I've got my cell with me."

Still aching from Gabriel's cane, Zoey headed to the coffee shop beneath a dull winter sun. Every step hurt. Cut. Stabbed. Despite the pain, she couldn't help but think about how good it felt when Josiah held her that time. So many men had touched her in so many ways last night, but this felt different.

It was pure. Simple. Innocent.

When Zoey finally got to Red Rooster, she saw Damien sitting in a booth. He looked out of place, surrounded by women with grey hair who were sipping burnt coffee and making flowery quilts. It felt more like a senior center than a coffee shop.

Damien hugged her. "I can't believe what Dad did to you last night."

"I don't want to talk about it," Zoey replied. "Let's talk about how we're going to get out of this—and bring that fucking cop down."

An old woman wearing an apron covered in ugly roosters interrupted them with a suspicious glance. "What can I get you two kids?"

They ordered a couple root beers and maple bars. After the

waitress walked away, Damien leaned in close and lowered his voice.

"Why're we meeting here?" he asked. "Shouldn't we have gone somewhere more private?"

"I'm not taking any more chances with your dad," Zoey said. "If he catches us trying to talk in secret, he'll know we're up to something again. This is probably the last place he'd expect us to meet."

Damien nodded in agreement.

"I should've told you this a long time ago," Zoey continued. "But Mom talked to someone right before that cop killed her. His name's Aidan, and he's a photographer at the paper. He contacted me a while ago, but I hung up on him. Good news is, I saved his number just in case. This guy promised Mom that he'd protect me and Camille."

Looking more suspicious than ever, the waitress shoved cans of soda and two plates of maple bars onto their table.

"Why was this guy talking to your mom?" Damien asked.

Zoey finished her doughnut in two bites and then continued.

"I don't know for sure. But he must've been on to something, right? There has to be a connection. I think he can help us."

Damien looked skeptical. "How could some random photographer help us?"

"Because Mom trusted him," Zoey said, tears forming beneath her eyes.

"I'm sorry," Damien replied. "I didn't mean it like that. I'm still confused, though. How can Aidan help us?"

This time, Zoey pulled her phone from her pocket and set it on the table.

"Because he doesn't have one of these pieces of shit," she said. "He's a pro, right? So I'm guessing his camera can shoot a lot farther than ours. With his help, we could actually do what we were trying to do with that stupid cell phone—capture those assholes in the act. Maybe that's what Mom had in mind all along."

Damien looked out the window for a while.

"You can't do it, Zoey. This is getting too dangerous. We already tried that once, and you could've gotten killed last night if Dad kept hurting you."

"I don't want to do this either, Damien," Zoey said. "You think I like any of this shit? But at this point, I don't know what else to do. When we tried running away, your dad kidnapped us. When Mom tried to help, he had someone murder her. And when I tried calling the cops... Aidan is our last fucking hope."

The waitress walked back to their table.

"Anything else you kids need? We've got a quilt show later this afternoon, so I can't have you loitering around here too long."

Damien paid the bill and walked outside with Zoey. She started to talk, but then he kissed her on the lips. Too stunned to speak, she just stood there, letting him.

"What was that for?" Zoey asked.

"I don't want anything else to happen to you," Damien replied. "I've never met anyone like you before, someone who cares so much for other people—like your sister. That's what I love about you. And that's why I'm so scared of this idea."

Zoey didn't know how to respond, so she just stared at the ground.

"Do you..." Damien started to ask. "Never mind."

"What?"

"Nothing. Well, I guess I just need to know. Do you like Josiah?"

Zoey's stomach lurched.

"I don't know," she said. "I mean, I've known him forever. Why are you even asking me that?"

"I don't know either," Damien replied. "Actually, I do. And I just think you can do so much better. Josiah lives in a trailer park, for crying out loud. There's no future there. Plus, he'll never understand you—us—and this world we live in. But I do. We're in this together, and once we get out of it together, I want you to come with me–"

"Stop it, Damien. I can't deal with this right now. I need to get back to–"

"To where, Zoey? You don't need to live with him. Come stay with me."

Zoey shook her head. "I can't do that. Mom wanted me and Camille to stay with Jo's parents."

"What happens when he finds out?" Damien asked. "How do you think he'll respond? He won't be able to handle the truth. But I'll always love you for who you are, no matter what happens."

For the first time in her life, she felt grown up. Respected. Maybe even loved.

Zoey told Damien goodbye and walked back to Josiah's trailer. He and Camille were doing some homework on the couch, so she joined them. But before long, Zoey grew tired again. As she lay her head on Josiah's shoulder, she thought about how truly different he and Damien were. Josiah was young and naïve, while Damien was mature and savvy. Josiah had spent his whole life in rural La Pine; Damien grew up in urban Seattle.

Both listened to her. Both cared for her. And both loved her. Well, maybe not Damien. Zoey wondered if she could ever trust and love the son of a pimp—even if he could relate to her. Deep down, Zoey knew that someday soon she would have to make a choice between them, between two very different worlds and lives.

But for now, she just wanted to hear the heater hum and fall asleep in Jo's arms.

———————

The next day, Zoey walked to school with Camille and Josiah under an unusually warm winter sky.

The sun had finally started to thaw some of the snow that piled up on sidewalks in heaps of grey slush, but Josiah reminded her that winter would be back soon, probably with renewed vengeance. She cursed under her breath.

Once Zoey got to school, she found a seat in Mr. Brookstone's class. Ivy—Leah—walked in a minute later and sat down right in front of her. Zoey started to sweat. Her thighs ached. Each face from the motel shot back into her mind. She stood up to leave, but just then Mr. Brookstone walked into class.

"We're going to discuss *Oliver Twist* today," her teacher said. "This is another great work by Dickens. As you know, the main character is a young boy who slaves away in a workhouse but finally escapes to the streets of London. While we could spend a whole year studying this story, one of my favorite characters is Nancy, the teenage prostitute."

Ivy glanced back at Zoey as he said those words. Nobody else seemed to notice.

"Now, who can tell me how Nancy joined the Artful Dodger's gang?" Mr. Brookstone asked.

Even though Zoey had only skimmed a few chapters this time, she had read the book on her own years ago and remembered sympathizing with Nancy.

"Someone *recruited* her," Zoey said, emphasizing that word as she kept her eyes trained on Ivy. "She came to the gang as a teenage girl. While the boys picked pockets, she sold her body to raise money for Fagin and her boyfriend, Sikes."

"Very good," Mr. Brookstone replied as he took off his glasses and walked up to Zoey. "And what kind of relationship did they have?"

This time, Ivy raised her hand. Their teacher seemed surprised, but he let her answer.

"He beat her," Ivy said as she glanced at Zoey. "He beat everybody, including his dog Bull's Eye. But he was really mean to Nancy."

Zoey shifted uncomfortably in her seat.

"So why didn't Nancy just run away?" Mr. Brookstone asked. "Why not just take off and be done with the life?"

"Because she cared for Oliver," Zoey said, staring right back at Ivy. "She wanted to help him escape."

Her teacher seemed thrilled that more than one student was talking for once in his class, so he let the conversation continue.

"And what happened to Nancy, in the end?" Mr. Brookstone asked.

Zoey swallowed hard.

"He killed her," Ivy said, looking right into Zoey's eyes this time. "For ratting him out."

Their teacher nodded. "Yes, that's one of the saddest chapters in the book."

As Mr. Brookstone continued talking, Zoey found the description of that brutal murder. But then Zoey read a passage right after that scene:

Of all bad deeds that, under cover of the darkness, have been committed within wide London's bounds since night hung over it, that was the worst. Of all the horrors that rose with an ill scent upon the morning air, that was the foulest and most cruel.

The sun—the bright sun, that brings back, not light alone, but new life, and hope, and freshness to man—burst upon the crowded city in clear and radiant glory. Through costly-colored glass and paper-mended window, through cathedral dome and rotten crevice, it shed its equal rays. It lighted up the room where the murdered woman lay. It did.

He tried to shut it out, but it would stream in.

Zoey looked back up again at Ivy, but the girl was glaring at Mr. Brookstone.

"Now, some of you may think this sort of thing only happened a long time ago," their teacher said. "After all, prostitution has been called 'the world's oldest profession.' But unfortunately, it still goes on today. Thousands of kids all across the country are in danger of becoming like Nancy."

Zoey re-read that last sentence after the murder scene about the sun pouring through the shutters to expose Nancy's death:

He tried to shut it out, but it would stream in.

Zoey couldn't handle it anymore. She stood up, walked to Ivy's desk and pointed her finger at the girl who had betrayed them to Gabriel.

"Sikes couldn't shut out the light," Zoey said. "And neither can *him*."

When Zoey, Camille and Josiah got back from school, Marge greeted them with a meal of microwaved hot dogs and canned beans.

"Thanks, Marge," Zoey said after she shoved the last spoonful of beans into her mouth.

"You're welcome, dear. Now, who's ready for some Hold 'Em? It's been too long since we've played some games around here as a family."

"What's Hold 'Em?" Zoey asked.

Josiah's dad, Bill, rolled his lazy eyes. "Please say you're shitting me. Everybody's played Hold 'Em."

Bill shrugged as he grabbed a bag of cheese puffs and began shoving them into the cave of his mouth. For the next few hours, Zoey's worries faded as she played poker. At first she didn't appear to understand the difference between a spade and a diamond, but by midnight she had stolen all of Josiah's and Camille's money.

"The girl's a natural," Bill said. "Maybe you should join me and the boys down at the Legion on Monday nights."

"Don't listen to the old fool," Marge said. "You'd much rather play Bingo with me and the ladies on Thursdays. At least we're civilized."

After a few more rounds, Zoey beat Marge.

"Now you're really shitting me," Bill said. "It's just between you and me, missy."

For the next hour, everyone watched as Zoey and Bill checked, raised, called and took each other's chips.

"All in," Zoey said on her last hand.

"Seriously?" Bill asked as a cheese puff drooped from his mouth. "You're bluffing."

Zoey winked at him.

"Fine," Bill replied as he shoved the rest of his poker chips to the center of the table with his chubby white fingers. "All in. What you got?"

"Show me yours first."

Bill revealed a full house, king high.

Zoey sighed. "Well, I was close. I've also got a full house—but ace high."

"Good Lord," Marge said as Josiah laughed and Bill cursed. "You've beat my husband for the first time in who knows how long. And to think you've never played poker."

"Oh, I've played a few hands," Zoey said.

After they cleared the table, Zoey and Camille got ready for bed. She hadn't felt this happy in such a long time. It was good to play games with a real family. She told Josiah goodnight, crawled onto her cot and started falling asleep until her phone buzzed with another text:

Meet @ 10. Got 2 jons.

Zoey didn't want to go, but she knew they had to convince Gabriel everything was fine if she was going to contact Aidan. So after checking to see if Marge and everyone else was asleep, Zoey and Camille snuck out of the trailer and made their way to the motel once again.

She turned her two tricks in ten minutes. They just wanted blow jobs, which made her work so much quicker. Zoey stepped outside her room and sat down on the cold concrete to eat what Gabriel had left the girls: a couple of Hot Pockets, a plastic jug of vodka and a pack of cheap cigarettes. Zoey inhaled the smoke deep into her lungs and took another hit of meth. Her whole body began to relax.

"Well, if it ain't the new bitch," Jasmine said as she plopped down next to her. "Just finish your trick, Iris?"

Zoey nodded.

"How was he?"

"Excuse me?" Zoey asked.

"I mean, how was he? Big cock? Cum fast?"

"I don't really want to talk about it."

"Oh come on," Jasmine said as she stole a swig of her vodka. "I just finished up with a real pussy. This bitch was so small I could've put his whole package in my mouth. Shit, I barely licked him before he came all over the place. The bastard had the balls to tell me to swallow, but I wasn't eatin' that shit. He had one rank cock."

"I feel sick," Zoey said.

"Good, you can give me your other Hot Pocket."

She shoved her food over to Jasmine, who swallowed it whole.

"Look at these bitches," Ivy said as she and Camille came out of their rooms at the same time. "What're you doing?"

"Swappin' stories," Jasmine said. "But little Iris here doesn't want to play. She's still too shy."

"That's too bad," Ivy said. "I just had the weirdest trick. This cocksucker wanted me to finger him until he came. I spent twenty minutes up his ass, but he finally gave up in anger and left."

"That's fucked up," Jasmine said. "But that's still not as bad as Teddy."

Ivy and Jasmine chuckled as Zoey and Camille shrugged their shoulders.

"Who's Teddy?" Zoey asked.

"This john came in wearing a suit," Jasmine said. "I thought he was like all the other pricks who work downtown. But he was wearing a bear costume underneath—and he brought another one for me to wear. Wanted us to do it like animals. I told him to get the fuck out. Said I wasn't doin' that shit."

The girls shared a few more stories until their sides hurt from laughing. Then they sat in silence, smoking their cigarettes. The sound of footsteps killed the quiet.

"Shit, someone's coming," Ivy said. "Hide the crank."

"What's so funny?" Damien asked as he appeared on the motel landing.

"Nothing," Ivy said. "Just having some girl talk."

"Well, get back to work. You're wasting time."

Ivy and Jasmine scurried back to their rooms. Zoey and Camille started to walk away, but Damien stopped them. "Where are you going?"

"I thought we just had two tricks tonight," Zoey said.

"You did," Damien replied with a whisper. "But I overheard my dad talking on the phone. He's arranged your next client. This isn't just any john. He's paying big money to do you at the truck stop. His name's Jacob Combs—and he's a social worker with the county."

Zoey froze. "Camille, go home right now. I'll take care of this."

For the first time, Zoey called Aidan.

CHAPTER 2

Aidan was just getting ready for bed when he got a call from Zoey.

"Still want to help us?"

"Of course."

"Good, then you need to do exactly what I say. Mom trusted you, but if I ever get the feeling you're trying to fuck with me or my sister, I swear to God I'll make you pay for it. Got it?"

He was too shocked to say anything.

"Now, I don't give a shit about your story or whatever you're hoping to get out of this," Zoey said. "My sister and I will only work with you on one condition—that you free us. Are we clear?"

Aidan couldn't believe he was taking orders from a teenage girl, but he agreed.

"So here's how it's going to work," Zoey continued. "My next client is a social worker, Jacob Combs. I need you to catch him. He's been supplying girls like my sister to our pimp, and he's not the only supplier either."

"I know," Aidan said. "I did some research on Jacob. I also have proof that a school records administrator has been providing girls to your pimp."

"Walter," Zoey said. "What kind of proof?"

Aidan told her about his tape recorded message.

"Good," Zoey said. "Now, if we can just catch Jacob on camera tonight, we'll have proof against his two main suppliers."

Aidan thought for a moment.

"Let me get this straight," he said. "You want me to take pictures of a man having sex with you?"

"Exactly."

"That's insane. You need to call the cops about this, not some photographer."

"I can't call the cops."

"Why the hell not?"

"Because I already tried that, and one of them works for my pimp. He'll kill us if we ever try calling the cops again. Or even finds out you and I talked."

Aidan sighed into the phone.

"I don't believe you. Listen, Zoey, one of my best friends is a deputy. And if there was anything going on like this, he'd know."

"Or would he?" Zoey asked. "What's your friend's name?"

"Briggs."

Aidan could hear cursing on the other end of the line.

"That's him," Zoey said. "That's the fucker who killed our mom."

Every skeptical warning bell went off in Aidan's head. That couldn't be true. Zoey had to be wrong. Or lying.

"How do you know?"

"Because he came to our motel," Zoey said. "And watched my pimp rape me."

For a long time, Aidan remained silent. He didn't want to believe Zoey, but her words made his skin crawl.

"All right, what time?"

"Meet me at Baldy's. Now."

———————

Aidan got to Baldy's just before midnight and sat down in a booth.

The waitress brought him some coffee. Aidan cleaned his telephoto lens and glasses one last time. Just to be sure. While waiting for Zoey, he couldn't help but think of every interaction he'd had with Briggs recently. True, the deputy had given him a lot of background information, including Leah's name. But maybe that was just his cover. His alibi.

Ade, you've got to be more careful. I don't want you to get hurt.

The cabin. The snake. The note.

His phone rang. "He's here," Zoey said. "What're you wearing?"

Aidan jolted back to the present and headed outside. "I've got a black North Face jacket on. Why?"

"You see the black Buick that just pulled up to the left of you?"

Aidan whipped his head around to find the girl as he stepped out into the parking lot. "Are you stalking me?"

"Well, you kind of stand out," Zoey said. "Now, do you see the car or not?"

"Yeah."

"Good, do you also see that old semi-truck parked at the other end of the lot?" Zoey asked. "Hide behind that while you take your pictures."

Aidan had no choice but to obey. He darted across the blustery lot to that semi as fast as his legs could move in the snow. Aidan hid behind the truck. Adjusted his glasses. Attached his telephoto lens. And aimed it at the Buick.

That's when he first saw her.

The girl drifted slowly toward the car, a black hood hiding her small frame. Aidan zoomed in closer. She climbed inside and uncovered her hood, revealing a face that looked so young. He took his first shot as the man handed the girl some cash, relying on the dim light of the lot.

Click.

He kissed her.

Click.

He took her shirt off.

Click.

He took her bra off.

Aidan froze. He couldn't believe what he was seeing. A grown man was undressing a young girl. It made him sick. Then it made him mad. He attached his external flash and raced up to the Buick. Despite the cold, Aidan was now sweating. His finger trembled as he touched the small black button on his camera.

Click. Click. Click.

For less than a second, the dark night turned bright as day, and Jacob's eyes turned from ecstasy to agony. Aidan knew those photos wouldn't turn out well because of the car window, but that didn't matter, because the man fell backwards out the door without his pants. Aidan took the liberty of snapping a few more shots that made the man's bare ass glow bright as the pale moon.

All of Aidan's journalistic training told him to put the story first, to keep his eyes fixed on the camera and record reality instead of trying to change it.

Fuck it. I'm not going to let this happen.

For the first time, Aidan put his camera down. He walked right up to Jacob with his hidden tape recorder as Zoey jumped out of the car and put her clothes back on. Aidan had the strongest urge to punch Jacob in the face, but decided to wait. At least for now.

Jacob's shaved head turned bright red.

"Who are you?" the social worker asked, looking back and forth between him and Zoey. "You some kind of cop?"

"No," Aidan said. "But I'm your worst fucking nightmare."

Jacob shivered. "What're you going to do with those photos? My wife, my kid, I don't know what they'll say."

"Here's what I'll say," Aidan continued. "You've got two choices, you little prick. Either you tell me some information, or I mail these photos to that wife and kid of yours."

Jacob sank into the snow.

"I never meant to get involved with this," Jacob said. "Her pimp blackmailed me. Sent a cop to threaten me if I didn't help him."

That got Aidan's attention. "What cop?"

"He'll kill me if I say."

"These photos will kill your career—and your family."

Jacob cursed. "Briggs. Randy Briggs."

Aidan couldn't believe it. Everything he knew about Briggs, everything they'd done together, was a lie. A fucking lie. He punched Jacob in the face.

"All right," Aidan said. "I won't do anything with these photos, but you'd better not supply any more girls from the workshop. If I hear otherwise, your wife and kid are in for a big surprise. You got me?"

Jacob nodded.

"Good," Aidan said. "Now get your pants back on, you piece of shit."

As the social worker got back into his car and skidded off into the night, Aidan aimed his camera again and took one last shot. Then he turned to Zoey and handed her his jacket.

"We got him," Aidan said. "Now let's catch Briggs."

CHAPTER 3

The sun was already rising on the high desert when Zoey returned to Josiah's trailer.

Jo and Camille were waiting for her at the door. She knew just by looking at his bleary eyes that he had been up all night, worrying. And she also knew that it was time to tell him the truth about her double life. He deserved to know.

In fact, Zoey decided not to even worry about her black eyeliner this morning. She wanted to tell him everything. About her dad. Leah. Gabriel. Walter. Jacob. And now Briggs. There was only so much Texas Hold 'Em she could play with his family before sneaking out into the night to have sex with strangers.

"We need to talk," Zoey said as she stepped inside and sat down by a plastic Christmas tree with white lights. It was the same one his family had owned since she was a little girl. She had so many memories playing by that tree and opening presents with her family and his.

"Just promise me one thing," Zoey continued. "No matter what I say, you'll still care for me and my sister and won't tell anyone—especially your mom."

Zoey could tell from Camille's face that she was begging her to stop. But she couldn't. Josiah had to know.

"I already told you that a long time ago," Josiah said.

"I know, but I need you to promise me again. I don't want anybody else to get hurt."

Josiah looked worried. "Now you're scaring me. Zoey, what's going on? I already know about the drugs."

"It's got nothing to do with drugs."

"What then?"

Zoey took a deep breath.

"I'm a prostitute," she said. "We both are."

To Zoey's surprise, Josiah just rolled his eyes.

"Come on, Zoey," he said. "That's not funny."

"I'm serious, Jo. But we didn't mean to get into this. It wasn't our fault."

"Seriously, stop it."

Zoey started crying. She didn't know what else to do. What else to say. Finally, the expression on Josiah's face began to change. It almost seemed to darken.

"What are you talking about?" he asked.

This time, Camille talked. "Zoey told you—it wasn't our fault. There's this guy–"

"Stop it," he said. "I... I can't... Please, just leave."

Zoey went to fall into Josiah's arms, but he backed away.

"Don't do this," Zoey said. "Please, we can't get out of this alone."

When Josiah spoke, his words felt like ice. "Leave."

As Zoey stepped back outside with Camille into the dawn, she didn't know where to go. Every last person in the normal world had turned their backs on them or betrayed them. So they headed for the highway.

Zoey didn't care that the rest of the world stared at her pale, sunken face while passing by on the road. She didn't care that they frowned on her for looking like a slob as they drove to work in suits with their fancy fucking coffee mugs. In fact, she didn't care if they all went to hell, because they weren't part of her world anymore.

Their world sucked. Their world hated her. Their world rejected her. Her world, the real world, was the truth. Only Damien could understand her now. So they headed back to Jugs.

———

As soon as they stepped inside the strip club, Gabriel started applauding.

"There they are," the pimp said. "Congratulations."

"What's going on?" Zoey asked.

"Nothing," Gabriel replied. "Other than the fact that I just finished counting our money and realized that you and your sister have raked in more than we made all last year. That means you're getting a little promotion tonight, Iris. We're buying you and Rose some new clothes."

The pimp looked at Camille, stared at her Princess Ariel shirt and then chuckled.

"God knows your sister needs to stop wearing those Disney shirts anyway," Gabriel continued. "Also, here's some more meth and jewelry from your Daddy."

Zoey was shocked, but skeptical. Maybe he was just fucking with her again. She turned to Damien. "I need to talk with you."

Damien led her into a back room of the club. "What's wrong?"

"Josiah just kicked us out."

"Bastard."

"Don't say that," Zoey said. "He just doesn't understand, but I don't know what to do now."

Damien looked around the room, probably to make sure Gabriel wasn't listening.

"I told you this would happen," he whispered. "Josiah doesn't get our world, this life. He never will, because he's not one of us. Come on, let's go back to my place."

After pleading with Gabriel for one day off from tricks, Zoey and Camille got in Damien's car and headed toward a newer section of homes in La Pine. Zoey saw what looked like blue fairies dancing in the yard of one home. She imagined garden gnomes scurrying about that yard with the fairies, just like she used to pretend as a child. Her mom was there, laughing. There were hot dogs and pitchers of strawberry lemonade, too.

But then the fairies became energy-efficient, solar-powered yard lights. And the garden gnomes were just black squirrels looking for yet another nut. Damien's car thudded over the railroad tracks. That reminded Zoey of her world, her life, the run-down convenience stores and rows of trailers bunched so tightly together she was sure no grass could grow.

Damien parked his car, walked the girls inside and shut the howling wind behind them. He poured himself a shot of cheap whiskey and made them some cups of cocoa with mini marshmallows.

"Sit down," he said, pointing to a couch so white it made her eyes hurt. She felt dirty just sitting on it.

As Damien boiled hot water and put in her favorite Nine Inch Nails CD, Zoey stared at his woodstove. Pictures of a younger man in blue jeans and plain T-shirts lined the top shelf, illuminated by lights dangling from pine beams above her.

"Is that your dad?" Zoey asked.

"That's him back in the day," Damien said as he sat between her and Camille on the couch and handed them steaming cups of the liquid sugar.

"Did he always used to dress that way?" Camille asked.

"Yeah, back when I was a little boy," Damien said. "My dad used to be a truck driver. He didn't start off wanting to be a pimp. I don't think anybody does, just like nobody's born wanting to be a prostitute."

Damien poured himself another shot of whiskey. His bright blue eyes became even more wolf-like as he grew angry and scratched at his rugged blond scruff.

"I fucking hate him," he said. "You know, Dad used to beat the shit out of my mom for being 'nothing but a whore' and me for 'not being man enough.' When I turned sixteen he took me to my first prostitute—just so I could 'become a man.'"

Damien slammed his whiskey bottle onto the glass coffee table, sending drops of the drink into the air and onto his white couch.

"But at least I've got some morals," he said. "He's raped so many girls I've lost count. I've never done that."

Zoey felt too sick to keep drinking hot chocolate. "Then why does your dad even let you work for them? Why not just disown you?"

"I don't know," Damien said. "Maybe deep down, he still cares for me. Maybe he still wants to be a good father."

Zoey shook her head. "You're not like him, you know."

"What the hell is that supposed to mean?" Damien asked. "You think I'm not man enough either?"

"No, I mean, you don't hurt me like the other guys. You're nice to me and my sister."

Damien stood up. "That's my goddam weakness. I hate it. I just want some fucking respect, you know?"

Zoey looked him straight in the eyes. "I respect you."

Damien smiled at her and Camille. That night, the three fell asleep on his couch. As her eyes began to droop, Zoey couldn't help but remember that, not long ago, she was falling asleep with Josiah on a couch by a space heater in his trailer.

Both listened to her. Both cared for her. And both loved her. Well, maybe not Josiah. Zoey wondered if he would ever be able to relate to her—and if she would ever be good enough for him. Deep down, Zoey knew that someday soon she would have to make a choice between them, between two very different worlds and lives.

But for now, she just wanted to hear the fire crackle and fall asleep in Damien's arms.

CHAPTER 4

The sun had already risen on the high desert when Aidan returned home.

Reina and Indie were waiting for him at the door. He knew just by looking at his wife's bleary eyes that she had been up all night, worrying. And he also knew that it was time to tell her the truth about his past with porn. She deserved to know.

But before he could say a word, Reina hugged him.

"What's this all about?" Aidan asked.

"Sit down, babe," Reina said.

Aidan was skeptical, but he obeyed. "There's something I need to tell you."

"Let me talk first," she said. "Indie, go back to your room."

"Am I in trouble?" their daughter asked with startled eyes.

"No, honey," Reina replied. "Mommy just needs to talk to Daddy."

"Daddy, you're in trouble," Indie said with a giggle.

Aidan and Reina both laughed. That eased the tension a little, although he could still sense some hesitation from his wife.

"Look, babe, this hasn't been easy," Reina said. "I still don't understand why you looked at those girls. Don't know if I ever will. But it was unfair to treat you like Charlie. At the end of the day, you were sorry—and he never was. So, I forgive you."

Aidan started to say something, but Reina kissed him. The feel of her lips on his and her tongue gently teasing his mouth drove him wild. He started to kiss and touch her back, but she pulled away.

"Calm down," she said. "There's something else I need to tell you. Briggs stopped by the house last night."

Aidan shuddered at the deputy's name.

"I know I've been hard on you about this assignment," Reina continued. "But after Briggs told me more about what you and Cal have been working on, I realized Zoey could be our daughter if circumstances were different. In fact, she could be anybody's daughter. So go help her."

That fucking bastard. Briggs knew. He knew everything. And now he was fucking with his own wife and daughter.

———

As soon as Aidan got to work, he and Cal updated Mitch with their latest facts about the administrator's school records and the social worker's abuse history.

Aidan was careful not to mention anything about Zoey or the photographs. He knew Mitch would go ape shit for getting too personally involved in his story.

"Good job, guys," Mitch said after listening to them. "I'm

impressed. We've at least got enough facts to run a story about the school records. Cal, get on that immediately. I want copy on my desk by four. But write only what you have solid documentation for. Can't risk a libel suit. Ade, get some shots at the school."

Mitch started to leave, but then came back.

"I know I'm always hard on you guys, but these really are some great stories," he continued. "If what you've said is true, we're talking about a major systems failure here in town. I mean, I knew it was getting bad when La Pine had to lay off some of their school counselors and resource officers, but this just keeps getting worse. I want you guys to expose this conspiracy and bring these fuckers down."

As soon as Mitch left, Aidan pulled Cal into an old darkroom and told him everything that had happened with Zoey and the social worker.

"Oh my God," Cal said as he looked through Aidan's photos. "Have you shown these to Mitch?"

"No, and we've got to keep it that way for now. I don't want him freaking out and killing the story. These pictures aren't exactly ethical or family friendly."

Cal laughed. "That's an understatement. Why didn't you call me?"

"I'm sorry. I should've done that. I just got so caught up in the shoot that I didn't even think twice about it."

Cal told him not to worry about it. Aidan thought about mentioning Briggs, but he couldn't bring himself to do that. He was a killer, and that secret had to stay between him and Zoey. Nobody else could know. Not Mitch. Not Cal. Not even Reina. It was up to him and Zoey now.

And they only had one shot left.

CHAPTER 5

Zoey knew she only had one last shot.

If she and Aidan made a single mistake, Briggs would kill them. So the next night, while waiting for another client at the motel, Zoey told her plan to Damien, Camille, Ivy and Jasmine. She had thought about not telling Ivy, because she still hated that bitch. But she needed her help. Everyone's help. They only had strength in numbers. Their pimp couldn't kill all of them or his business would die.

"Holy shit," Jasmine said. "That's brilliant, bitch. Can't believe we never thought of that before. Ivy, what do you think?"

Ivy took a drag of her cigarette that sent wisps of white smoke into the icy air. For a long time, she remained silent. Zoey knew this was it. She was taking a big risk telling them about their plan, but it wouldn't work without them. Either Ivy would join them—or rat them out.

"Fuck them," Ivy said. "Let's do this."

Zoey sighed with relief. She texted Aidan from a prepaid phone he had given her and told him to hide outside the motel in the spot they had discussed. Then Damien and the girls all joined Zoey in her motel room. She handed Jasmine a can of pepper spray.

As Zoey lay on the bed for her next client, everyone else got into position. Damien and Camille on the left side of the door. Ivy and Jasmine on the right.

Zoey began to shiver. Room 851 was always cold, but this time the shivering came more from fear than temperature. Zoey hoped Aidan was here. She hoped the girls would be quick enough.

Outside, Zoey could hear a car pull up. Bright headlights shone through the thin curtain, piercing the darkness.

Clank clank.

"You bitches ready?" Jasmine asked.

Clank clank. Clank clank.

"Let's fuck 'em."

Clank clank. Clank clank. Clank clank.

As soon as the man opened the door, Jasmine sprayed him in the eyes.

The man screamed as Damien punched him in the face, Ivy jammed her fingers into his eyes, Camille crushed his balls with her hand and Jasmine threw her weight against his thin body. The client crashed to the floor. They continued spraying him. Punching him. Kicking him.

Finally, Zoey got up from her bed and walked toward him. She stared at his bruised and bloody face. He was wearing a suit. Looked wealthy. Powerful. Maybe he'd just come from work. Or a wedding. Or a date.

But Zoey didn't give a shit. She lifted her right steel-toed boot high into the air and then brought it down with force like a bat onto his head.

The man groaned on the ground. Zoey started walking away, but then a rage she had never felt before rose up within her. She wanted him to pay. She wanted all of these bastards to pay. So she ran back to the man and kicked him again. And again. And again. The short tan carpet turned red. Jasmine tried pulling Zoey off, but she kept beating the man until he passed out.

"Holy shit," Jasmine said. "We just fucked up a client."

"Good," Zoey replied. "He fucked with the wrong girls."

Zoey dragged his limp body to a corner of the room and took a picture of his face. The man's skin was so swollen you couldn't even see his eyes. She took a picture and then sent it to Gabriel, using some of his own words against him.

Look @ ur client. Want me 2 delete these pics? Or do u want 2 see more clients like this?

Zoey knew he and Briggs would be at their motel room any minute. Running right into their trap. She texted Aidan and reminded him to get his best shot of her pimp and the deputy at the motel together. Exactly what the cops would need to charge Gabriel and Briggs.

A minute went by. Then two. Then three. Zoey wondered if they'd made a mistake. Maybe they wouldn't come after all. Maybe this whole plan was a mistake.

All of a sudden, Zoey heard a knock on the door. Josiah entered the room. He looked in shock at Damien, the girls and the bloody client in the corner.

"No," Zoey said. "No, no, no. Jo, what are you doing? You can't be here. They'll kill you."

"I'm here to get you," he said. "I should've done this a long time ago."

Without thinking, Zoey tried to shove him out the door.

"Stop," Josiah said. "It's my fault. I should've never kicked you out of our trailer. I had no clue you girls were actually forced into this."

"How'd you find us?" Zoey asked.

"I followed you to the motel," Josiah said. "Oh God, I'm so sorry, Zoey. Can you ever forgive me?"

This time, Zoey and Iris both stared at the floor, fighting each other in the same mind. She could feel that scaly insect crawling around in her brain again, cracking her even deeper into two halves. She looked back and forth between Damien and Josiah. Between her two worlds. Her two lives.

"Can you forgive me, Zoey?" Josiah asked again.

Zoey stared into those pale, ash grey eyes she had almost forgotten. At first she hated him. Her own green eyes became wild and violent like the sea. But then she felt sorry for him and remembered how much he had helped her along the way.

Before Zoey could answer, Aidan entered the room. Briggs and Gabriel followed right behind him, guns pointed at the back of his head. The pimp saw the client in the corner of the room and cursed.

"What the fuck," Gabriel said. "You kids are dead."

CHAPTER 6

Briggs forced everyone except for Zoey to stand up against the wall at gunpoint.

The deputy wasn't wearing his uniform. Thank God, he was off duty. Aidan had confirmed that before tonight, because they couldn't risk him hearing anything on Dispatch. It was a good sign their plan could still work.

Gabriel sat down on the motel bed and motioned for Zoey to join him. Gabriel began stroking Zoey's legs. She could tell he was getting turned on as his breathing became heavier.

"Get your hands off her," Josiah said.

"How do you know she doesn't like it?" Gabriel asked. "After all, it's how she makes a living now. And she's pretty damn good at it. But you wouldn't know, would you? You're still a virgin from what I hear. I'll bet you've been saving yourself for her."

Josiah lowered his eyes to the ground.

"Why?" Gabriel asked. "Josiah, do you know how many men this little bitch has been with? She'll never be good enough for you."

"It doesn't matter," he said. "I... I love her."

Gabriel laughed. "Well, isn't that nice. But at the end of the day, it's not about love, Josiah. It's about how good you are at fucking or getting fucked."

Camille started to panic. She flapped her hands uncontrollably, curled into a ball and screamed. Zoey reached out to calm her, but she only shrieked louder.

"It's OK Camille, you're OK," her sister said. "It's OK Camille, you're OK."

"You see what's happening?" Damien told Josiah. "She's having another one of her panic attacks because of boys like you who reject girls like them."

Josiah started to lunge at Damien, but Briggs forced him to back up.

Zoey looked at Aidan. He was staring outside the window, probably wondering—like her—where the cops were. They should have been here by now. Aidan was supposed to have called them outside the motel and told them everything. But maybe he never had the chance. Maybe Briggs got to him first.

"I have an idea," Gabriel said. "Let's settle this by making Zoey decide between you two."

The pimp smiled at her.

"Forget him," Josiah said. "I'm here for you now."

"Now?" Damien asked. "You're here for her now are you? Well, what about the time when she was honest with you, Jo? I heard you kicked her out onto the street. Right in the dead of winter. Some friend you are."

"I know I screwed up," Josiah said. "I'm sorry."

Damien laughed. "But you see, Jo, Zoey's never had to forgive me, because I've never hurt her. I love her for who she is—something you wouldn't understand because you're just a poor fucking redneck."

Josiah started to raise his fist, but Gabriel stopped him.

"Both of you, shut the fuck up," the pimp said. "The only one who can end this is her. Zoey, you have to choose. Tell me which one to shoot."

Zoey just stared at Gabriel.

"Dad, stop," Damien said. "What're you doing?"

"I don't care," the pimp replied. "I'm sick of this bullshit. She needs to decide which boy—and life—she wants. Once and for all."

"Stop it," Zoey said. "I can't do this."

"Then I'll just kill you," Gabriel replied. "So what's it going to be, Iris?"

Zoey looked back and forth between both boys. Then she saw Camille and thought of her mom, holding them by the space heater while singing them softly to sleep. And in that moment, Zoey knew her decision.

She gathered one last bit of strength to spit on Gabriel's face.

"Fuck you," Zoey said. "And fuck Iris. My name's Zoey, bitch."

Zoey hoped her death would be quick, but nothing happened. Gabriel just stood there. Then he lowered his gun and started laughing.

"Wow," the pimp said. "I underestimated you once again. But it doesn't matter anymore."

Gabriel nodded to Briggs. He smiled at Zoey and cocked his gun.

CHAPTER 7

The cops still hadn't shown up.

Zoey's mind raced like mad to think of every possible way they could escape. After all, it was seven against two. But Briggs and Gabriel had guns. There was nothing they could do about that fact. So she waited. And waited.

Between the blinds of the motel window, Zoey could see thick black clouds hovering over the high desert. The wind began to pick up. In desperation, Zoey thought about knocking Gabriel's gun out of his hand. But he seemed to sense her attack.

"Calm down, girl," Gabriel said. "I need you to save your energy for one last trick. Aidan, come here."

Camille screamed at Gabriel and raced toward him, but Briggs forced her to back up. Zoey looked at Aidan. At first he appeared defeated. But when she finally caught his gaze, she could see a fire burning in his eyes.

"Fuck you," Aidan said. "That's not going to happen. You'll have to kill me first."

Briggs laughed. "Well, look who finally decided to man up. But is your story really worth that, Ade?"

"It's not about my story anymore," Aidan said. "It's about doing the right thing. So go ahead. Pull the trigger. I just want to know why you weren't man enough to kill me before."

Briggs hurled Aidan to the ground and kicked him in the ribs.

He tried crawling away, but the deputy kicked him again in the face. Then Briggs grabbed Aidan by the throat and shoved him against the wall. The deputy's fingers snaked around Aidan's neck. Right before Zoey thought he would pass out, Briggs slammed him to the ground. After gagging several times, Aidan finally spoke.

"Why?" he asked.

"That's always the question, isn't it?" the deputy replied. "Now, I'm not going to lie. I got some good cuts of deals from people like Walter and Jacob. They paid me pretty well to turn a blind eye and not arrest them for supplying low-life scum like Zoey. But at the end of the day, do you know why I really did it?"

Aidan shook his head.

"Because there's no greater turn on," Briggs said. "There is no greater thrill in life than to see that look of horror on a young girl's face when she realizes what we're about to do to her."

Briggs glanced back and forth between Zoey and Aidan with a cruel grin.

"Man, I can't wait to read your obituaries in tomorrow's paper. What do you think they'll say about you, Aidan? I'm guessing something about how you raped some teens in a motel, killed them and then shot yourself. That's what my report will say anyway."

Knowing there was nothing else they could do, Zoey shut her eyes.

As Briggs walked up to her, Zoey wondered what she would see after death. For some reason, the first image that came to her mind was David Copperfield. Zoey smiled. Her teacher Mr. Brookstone was right—these characters were helping her keep hope, even at the very end. Zoey could still hear people screaming, but slowly their voices became quieter and the words of her favorite characters grew louder:

I hope that simple love and truth will be strong in the end, David Copperfield told her. *I hope that real love and truth are stronger in the end than any evil or misfortune in the world.*

Zoey felt the cold barrel on her forehead.

Another and better day is dawning, Uncle Tom said as he held her hand.

Zoey took one last breath.

The rest is silence, The Scarlet Pimpernel whispered into her ear. *Silence and joy for those who had endured so much suffering—yet found at last a great and lasting happiness.*

Right when Zoey's mind was about to go dark, she heard Briggs yelling.

Zoey opened her eyes and saw Camille clinging to Briggs'

back, her legs wrapped around his waist as she clawed at his neck and eyes with her long fingernails. Zoey couldn't believe her sister's strength. She dug deep into the deputy, drawing blood from his skin. Gabriel tried getting a good shot, but Briggs' head was too close to Camille's. Briggs tried tossing her off his back, but she dug even deeper. Ivy and Jasmine joined her. The last cut tore his neck so hard he dropped his gun.

Then Damien made a move. He dove for the pistol and aimed it at his father.

"Drop it, Dad," Damien said. "It's over."

"If I were you, I'd be very careful right now," Gabriel replied. "You don't know what you're doing, boy."

Damien stepped closer to his father, keeping his gun and eyes locked on Gabriel. Briggs had finally managed to pry the girls off him, but he was now rolling on the ground, trying to stop the blood that poured from his neck.

"You're wrong, Dad," Damien said. "For the first time in my life, I do know what I'm doing. These girls are finally free. And so am I."

Gabriel frowned. "What are you talking about?"

Aidan lifted up his shirt to reveal his tape recorder. "The cops will be here any second."

For a second, Gabriel hesitated, glancing back and forth between Aidan and his son.

Then he shot Damien. The bullet ripped through his son's neck and impaled the wall behind him. Zoey screamed. Josiah tried to grab the gun, but Gabriel reached it first. Damien writhed on the floor, blood gurgling from his neck.

"Please," Zoey said. "Let me help him. He's bleeding to death, for God's sake."

At that moment, the motel door cracked open. Sheriff deputies burst into the room with a SWAT team. They looked in shock at Briggs, but kept their focus.

"Drop the guns," an officer shouted.

Gabriel refused, wildly pointing it back and forth between Zoey and Aidan. She could tell the pimp was panicking. He could pull the trigger any second. She closed her eyes as a gunshot rang in her ears.

But then Zoey heard Gabriel screaming.

She saw him clawing at his leg that was bleeding from a bullet hole. The SWAT team swarmed around Briggs and Gabriel. Officers handcuffed both of them—trapping them once and for all. Paramedics raced toward Damien and the client, who was still passed out. The room started spinning and she fell to the floor. A deputy helped Zoey to her feet and wrapped a blanket around her.

Zoey looked over at Damien. He wasn't moving anymore.

"Is Damien OK?" she asked the deputy. "Will he make it?"

The man just hung his head. Zoey started crying and shaking as every possible emotion burned through her body like fire. The room started spinning again. The deputy gave her a sip of water.

"Drink this," he said. "It's over."

CHAPTER 8

A week later, Aidan woke early to the alarm on his cell phone. He sat up groggily in bed and glanced at the time. Six in the morning. Aidan tried getting up. But when he saw his wife lying naked next to him, he hit the snooze button and fell back to sleep. After another ten minutes, Aidan woke a second time to the alarm.

"Damn it," he said, striking the snooze button again as Reina rolled over and lay her hand on his chest. He caressed her back for a few minutes while thinking about his next story. Aidan started to get up, but then he remembered what day it was. He jumped out of bed, strode to the front porch and read the paper's top headline:

Public officials arrested in murder and sex-trafficking conspiracy

It was the story of his career. Newspapers across the country picked it up. He even got a call from an editor in Seattle about a possible job opportunity. Aidan and Cal had spent all week giving their photos, tape recordings and other evidence to the sheriff while preparing for their double-truck spread, complete with photos, charts, sidebars and memoirs of the victims—especially Ella. They also focused on the impact the arrests had on the school district, the sheltered workshop and the sheriff's office. But Aidan didn't care about that. Not now. He crawled back into bed. An hour later, his phone buzzed again, this time with a call from Mitch.

"Good morning," Aidan said.

"What the hell's good about it?" his editor asked. "We've got a huge hole for tomorrow's paper. Look, I know you and Cal worked your ass off this last week for today's story, but we need to move on. I need you guys to get something good out of WinterFest. Two stories already fell through."

Aidan looked at Reina. She smiled. It was time to set some limits. He was going to treat his wife to their favorite dinner spot on top of Mt. Bachelor and take her to see some films at the Tower Theatre. Maybe even take Indie to the High Desert Museum of animals and the Sun Mountain Fun Center. Anything aside from work.

"I'm taking the day off," Aidan said.

"Excuse me?" Mitch asked.

"Maybe more than one," Aidan replied. "In fact, I might take all of my vacation that I never get to use because I'm always covering stories for you at the last minute. I'm sorry, Mitch. But I need a break. I need to spend some real time with my family."

Mitch said a few four-letter words. Aidan told his editor

goodbye and then kissed his wife. She kissed him back. Before they knew it, they were making love again. Both moaned so loud that their daughter woke up and knocked on the door.

"Shit," Aidan said. He grabbed a blanket and covered them both.

"Mommy, is that you?" Indie asked. "I heard a weird noise."

"Yes, honey, it's me and Daddy," Reina said. "Go back to bed."

Aidan took off his glasses. While falling asleep with his wife beside him, he looked over at his satchel, laptop and camera lens lying on the nightstand next to Reina. Suddenly, that nervous feeling crept back and part of him still longed to look at porn again. Right here. Right now. Then he felt sick and wanted to clean his lens. But for the first time, he chose not to look or to clean.

For the first time, he felt free.

CHAPTER 9

A week later, Zoey woke early beneath clean cotton sheets. She was wearing a white shirt. Her black hoodie and steel-toed boots were lying on a chair next to her bed, looking clean for the first time in ages. The morning light streamed across her face through an open window as she sat up in bed. She could hear those red-tailed hawks screeching and downy woodpeckers chirping again among the ponderosa pines. Zoey's body ached all over, but it was the good kind of pain that comes from rest after a long ordeal. She started to get up, then fell right back into bed, staring at the light and feeling a calm wind blow across her face.

Someone knocked on the door. Zoey began to panic, wondering if it was her next client, Gabriel or Briggs. But then she remembered what day it was. It was her seventh day free at Harriet's Hideaway, a safe house for survivors of sex trafficking. She just wished Damien had lived to see her make it here.

"Good morning, Miss James," a woman said as she walked into the room and checked her vitals. "How are you feeling today?"

"Exhausted," Zoey said.

"That's normal. How are your headaches?"

"Still have them, but they're hurting less and less."

"Good, Miss James," the woman said. "You and the other girls still have a long way to go, especially with the withdrawals. You can't expect to recover from everything overnight. But you're making progress. And in the meantime, you have a visitor. He just got done talking to your sister down the hall."

Josiah walked through the door with some flowers and that broad grin on his face. This time he wasn't wearing his orange hunting cap, and his hair actually looked somewhat combed over his freckled forehead. He also had on a new flannel shirt. Josiah sat next to her on the bed. Neither spoke for a while, but just smiled at each other.

"Mom and Dad are with Camille right now," Josiah said. "They've been crying all morning. I think they feel guilty for not knowing what was actually going on."

Josiah started tearing up himself. "I'm sorry for..."

"Stop," Zoey said as she tried sitting up in bed, but gave up out of weakness. "I already forgave you."

Josiah kissed her. And then he got up from the bed.

"Get some rest," he said. "We've got lots of Blizzards to get caught up on."

After Josiah left, Zoey walked into the bathroom and took a hot shower. For a long time, she stared at her razor lying next to the soap. Then she got ready to smear on another dark glob of eyeliner beneath her left lid. Part of her still wanted to end it all.

Right here. Right now. But for the first time, she chose not to cut or to hide.

For the first time, she felt free.

There are dark shadows on the earth,
But its lights are stronger.

— Charles Dickens —

JOIN THE CAUSE

The International Labour Organization estimates that there are 20.9 million victims of forced labor and human trafficking, including 5.5 million children. In the United States alone, the National Human Trafficking Resource Center hotline has received reports of at least 14,588 sex trafficking cases since 2007.

Those are harsh facts. But your purchase of *The Black Lens* makes a difference, because the author is donating 10 percent of his earnings from this book to organizations that battle modern slavery.

Aside from reading, you can also join the cause by volunteering for local, national or international organizations. If you have any information about a potential trafficking situation, please contact the National Human Trafficking Resource Center at 1-888-373-7888 or text BeFree (233733).

END THE DEMAND

Human trafficking is big business. Forced labor in the private economy generates $150 billion in illegal profits per year—with $99 billion of that coming directly from commercial sexual exploitation.

Like any business, trafficking relies on the law of supply and demand. While many factors fuel the demand, pornography is a key part of the problem.

During interviews with 854 women in prostitution in nine countries, 49 percent said pornography was made of them while they were in prostitution, and 47 percent were upset by tricks' attempts to make them do what the tricks had previously seen in pornography.

For information on how you can help end the demand, check out Pure Hope Coalition, Fight the New Drug and the Chicago Alliance Against Sexual Exploitation.

ENGAGE THE ARTS

The following essay is based on an interview between Christopher Stollar and Nick Nye, the lead pastor of Veritas Community Church.

What inspired you to write this book?

I wrote *The Black Lens* because it's a story that must be told.

Personally, I spent more than three years researching sex trafficking and interviewing prostitutes, police officers and social workers. One of the women I met with told me she got enslaved in an upper-middle class suburb of Detroit at age fifteen. Fifteen!

And she's not alone. In the United States, the National Human Trafficking Resource Center hotline has received reports of at least 14,588 sex trafficking cases since 2007. That's a harsh fact.

But this book can make a difference. Not only will it tell a great story, but it will also help raise awareness of modern slavery.

While this topic has received more press in the last few years, many people still don't think sex trafficking happens much in the United States. But that couldn't be further from the truth. A few recent books and movies have drawn attention to this crime, but no popular fiction so far has focused solely on trafficking in America.

That's where *The Black Lens* can help.

Why did you choose fiction as your genre?

I chose fiction as my genre because I love the art of storytelling.

British author C.S. Lewis once wrote, "Art ... has no survival value; rather it is one of those things which give value to survival."

Fiction is a form of art, so it too has no inherent survival value. But novels can give value to survival in unique and powerful ways. Think of the impact behind books like *Uncle Tom's Cabin* or *To Kill a Mockingbird*. Those novels affected so many people's views of race and slavery in ways that no other medium could.

One of my favorite books in the Bible is Esther, because it reads like a work of modern fiction. You've got a strong female heroine, romantic suspense and even a murder plot. But most interestingly, the book doesn't mention God once. Yet for those who have eyes to see, every sentence in the story points to God and gives value to the idea of surviving suffering.

What do Christians have to contribute in arts and specifically writing?

As created beings, Christians have so much to contribute to the arts—especially in the area of writing. For centuries, believers were at the forefront of art and culture. The Catholic Church sponsored some of the most famous artists of all times, such as Michelangelo.

But for decades, Christians have retreated from the arts. I don't know all the reasons, but Swiss author Francis Schaeffer once wrote: "I am afraid that as evangelicals, we think that a work of art only has value if we reduce it to a tract."

When you consider recent Christian novels or books, most of them don't take sin seriously. They focus so much on the truth of grace that they hide from the truth of evil. And yet if you spend any time reading the Old Testament, you discover that it's filled with descriptions of evil. You've got rape, incest—even torture. None of these authors glorified those crimes or described them in graphic detail, but they also didn't shy away from them either.

Why? Because they were trying to contrast the depth of man's evil with the depth of God's grace.

One of my favorite Christian authors is Flannery O'Connor, who became famous for her dark, brutal and violent short stories. She once wrote: "The truth does not change according to our ability to stomach it."

That's great advice for every Christian writer. We need to contrast both good and evil if we want to have any chance at engaging the world with our words.

As C.S. Lewis once wrote, "The world does not need more Christian literature. What it needs is more Christians writing good literature."

THANK THE DONORS

T*he Black Lens* exists because of readers like you.

This book would also not have been possible without support from The Great Author, Veritas Community Church and the following donors who pledged $3,694 on Kickstarter to bring this project to life—surpassing the original goal by 48 percent.

Advocates

Matthew Long

Walter Fountain

Jawella Hess

Terry and Deanna Stollar

Glenn A. Lowy

Ron and Jan Meissner

Jonathan Anderegg

Luke and Shelby Brooks

Robert Titus

Melinda and Freeman Troyer

Kathleen Cochran

David Eastman Jr.

Brad and Melissa Pauquette

Stu Martinez

Betty Nauratil

Partners

Brandon and Carmen Cupples

A. Harley

Nick Bowsher

Anthony

Tracy Thatcher

Amanda Lotycz

Michael Iles

Joe Rose

Jean Cherniss

Jennifer Allen

Natalie Siston

Paul Rose

Nick Nye

Derek Nicol

Kirby Nielsen

For the full list of donors, go to www.christopherstollar.com.

MEET THE AUTHOR

Christopher Stollar is a former reporter with a master's degree in journalism. He conducted more than three years of research on sex trafficking for *The Black Lens*, including interviews with survivors, social workers and police officers.

The author and his wife have also volunteered with several nonprofit organizations that help victims get off the streets and survivors find safe homes. This in-depth knowledge lends realism to *The Black Lens*.

Christopher wrote this manuscript because he wanted to tell a great story that also sheds light on the dark underworld of sex trafficking. That's why he has dedicated ten percent of his earnings to nonprofit organizations that fight the sex trade, such as She Has a Name. When the author isn't writing, reading or volunteering with his church and anti-trafficking organizations, he loves spending time with his wife and daughter in Columbus,

Ohio. He also enjoys a good pint of dark beer.

Contact Christopher by email at blacklensnovel@gmail.com. The author is available for interviews and as an expert resource.

Learn more at www.christopherstollar.com.

DISCLAIMER

The Black Lens is a work of fiction. The names, characters, crimes, incidents, school district, county workshop, sheriff's office and certain locations are the products of the author's imagination, and are not to be construed as real. While the author was inspired in part by actual events, none of the characters in the book are based on any actual people. Any resemblance to persons living or dead is entirely coincidental and unintentional.

CPSIA information can be obtained at www.ICGtesting.com
Printed in the USA
BVOW02s1427120516

447642BV00003B/27/P